Nick Storie
Time Will Kill You

<u>Critic comment 2019</u>: I was reading a few older books from my mother's collections. This was among them.

I do critiques of many books for groups, and make recommendations as to what I feel is worthy of buying. I must admit that more than half of the things I'm asked about are *not* worth the price – even many of the free eBooks are overpriced. It is far too easy to self-publish today, and works of value are far too often totally overlooked.

I have not seen manuscripts as well-worth reading as this one in two years, if not longer.

There are no descriptions of bloody, vulgar violence, no karate matches so far from reality as to become humorous, no vulgarity for the sake of vulgarity. In short, just a very able and likeable cop doing his job.

This is the first I have read by Moulton, and will not be the last. I like all the people at South Station. They are human. If all of the Nick Storie Mysteries are of the quality of these, I would recommend them as a TV series.

I am contacting Moulton through his publisher and suggesting, considering how today's market is for shorter works, that *Time Will Kill You* be offered as a single work.

Joyce Anniston Levenstahl

Contents

About the author

CD Moulton has traveled extensively over much of the world both in the music business, where he was a rock guitarist, songwriter, and arranger, and in an import/ export business. He has been everything from a bar owner to auto salvage (junkyard) manager, longshoreman to high steel worker, orchid grower to landscaper, tropical fish farmer to commercial fisherman. He started writing books in 1983 and has published more than 175 books as of January 1, 2013. His most popular books to date are about research with orchids, though much of his science fiction and fantasy work has proven popular. He wrote the CD Grimes, PI series and the Det. Nick Storie series, among other works.

He now resides in Puerto Armuelles, Panamá, where he writes the Clint Faraday mystery series, plays music with friends – and pursues his favorite ways to spend his time: beach bum and roaming the mountain jungles doing botanical research. He has lately become involved in fighting for the rights of the indigenous people, who are among his closest friends, and in fighting the extreme corruption in the courts and police in Panamá.

He offers the free e-book, *Fading Paradise*, that explains what he has been through because of the corruption.

CD is the discoverer of the Chadam protocol for curing cancer. Facebook page Ambrosia peruviana for cancer.

Jane Warfield sighed, held the sheet of plastic over her head and ran for the little car parked (naturally!) clear out by the road – as far from the door to her office as she could get.

Well, she knew it might rain when she parked it there. No one was to blame but herself, so grin and bear it!

She had the key ready, opened the door, and slid in under the wheel. She removed the package from under the flap in her purse and slipped it back under the seat, started the car, and headed into the storm. It would be good to get home where it was warm and dry. The biggest problem with this business was days like this. Nothing had gone right all day. It wouldn't start now.

Maybe she'd make a profit. It was about time! That was one turkey who was going to wake up wondering what the hell had smacked him! Sleazeball jerk!

She pulled into the garage at her condo, swore at the car in her space, and pulled on into the open visitor's area, found a reasonably dry spot, parked, and got out. The elevator was empty, for a rare change. She managed to get to the sixth floor without having to listen to old lady Winton's latest aches and pains or to old man Robert's suggestively vulgar insulting little innuendo-filled sexist diatribes.

No one saw her going up to 604 to open it. She went inside, swearing at the open window that had let just enough rain blow in to make the rug smell like a dirty wet dog. She was certain she'd closed it.

Something was definitely very wrong here! Someone had been in her apartment and had left that window open! Why? Why would anyone open the window? It was a sheer six-story drop outside.

The desk was a mess.

She went to the phone to call the manager. This had to stop

– and right now! She couldn't have this kind of thing, not in her business.

She heard a noise in the bedroom and turned.

Then, nothing.

Chapter one

"Line two, Nick!" Vic, desk sgt. on duty at the south station said on the intercom eight minutes after Homicide Det. Lt. Nathaniel "Nick" Storie came on duty. Nick picked up the receiver, punched line 2, and said, "Storie. Homicide."

"This is Lucille Byrd. I'm manager of Skyline Royalview Condos on the island," came back. "I heard an odd noise over the phone, then the woman, Jane Warfield, sort of gurgled and the line went dead. I called back and didn't get an answer and came up here. She was laying by the phone, dead! There's a piece of rope around her neck!"

"Don't touch anything! Be sure no one enters the room!

"You are calling from her phone?"

"Yes, I ... oh, dear! Someone hung it up! The killer! And I ... oh, dear!"

"The killer was probably wearing gloves, but be sure that no one else goes into that room! What is the number?"

"The apartment? Six oh four."

"We're on the way!"

Nick called forensics to give Dr. Tiny Menthorne the address, and headed out for the condo. It was a dreary dismal day – or night, if you considered the light level. Nick came on duty at six and it was already dark, what with the cloud cover at this time of year.

The condo building was pretty much like any other in the area. Overpriced and poorly maintained. Probably had a lot of phony snob appeal. People could brag about how much they got stuck for the place.

Nick noticed the parking space labeled #604 was empty. He parked his Trans Am in it and headed for the elevator to the left of #600 and punched for 6. The car stopped at four and a sour older woman got on, said she hated this kind of weather. It made her arthritis hurt and her sinuses clog. She said she should have moved to Arizona instead of Florida, with which Nick agreed. She didn't know how to take that, so didn't say anything else.

Nick got off the elevator, noticing the wet marks on the strip rug by the doors. Three sets. A woman was standing beside the door of #604. She introduced herself as the manager. Everybody called her Lucy – and she'd never get over going in and finding her like that.

"I'll look over the scene and come back out here until the coroner arrives. You say she called you on the phone, made a gurgling noise, and the line went dead?"

"Well, she hung it up. It didn't go dead in the sense there was nothing there. I called back and she didn't answer, so I came straight up."

Nick nodded and went inside. The body was laying beside the phone stand, about three feet from a narrow door he could see a bed and chair through. There wasn't much sign of a struggle.

The victim was attractive, of medium height and weight, had dark hair, and was wearing a business suit.

Nick quickly went through the rooms, noticing very little out of sync. Details, such as the damp rug under the window. The window was closed and locked. That would have to be explained. The frosted glass didn't show anything from inside. He opened it to look out, noting the six story drop to the outside parking lot. There were only two cars and a minivan out there.

There was a little red plastic rain hood on the straightback chair by the entrance. Nothing else of any significance. There was a wet spot beside it where something else had been.

Nick saw she wore a little watch in a pendant. It was face down. He turned it over. It was an older mainspring-operated type, possibly fairly valuable. It had stopped at 5:41. That probably meant nothing. She might have worn it simply as jewelry. She had a wrist watch that read the same as his own. Nick merely noted it.

Tiny soon came in immediately behind Frog Forest, the forensics ace photographer, who was panning around the room with a camcorder. Nick didn't have to make any suggestions to Frog. He wouldn't miss an inch. Nobody in the business was better than Frog.

"Lovely evening, Nick," Tiny (6'6" and 345#+) greeted. "It looks like it might clear up next week – or the next!

"Jane Arlene Warfield, PI, if you didn't know. She's had a run-in or two with Ed on a B and E, one a few days ago. The guy suddenly dropped all charges after talking to her privately for about one half minute or less. He all of a sudden 'remembered' he'd said something to her she might have interpreted as permission.

"I was there because a woman had OD'ed in an apartment a few doors farther along the hall. Ed was called about the same time and came over with his crew. She was inside and the guy – what was his name? Knowles!

"So anyhow, Ed's crew found her hiding in the restroom. She talked to Knowles, and he said it was all a big mistake. Ha, ha!

She found something."

"Thanks, Tiny. That might help to explain why something's not here that should be. I already spotted a couple of things. I'll need a very close time of death if you can give it."

"Pretty close. It was less than two hours I can tell you from this far away."

Nick went out into the hall and asked Lucy if Jane owned a car, used taxis, or had some other arrangements.

"She has a car. It'll be in the space downstairs marked six oh four. She was a private detective. She had to have her own transportation. It's one of those foreign things. They all look alike to me. Sort of dark maroon."

"What kind of work did she do? Divorce?"

"No. She wouldn't take that kind of thing. She found people and property, I think. Insurance claims. That sort of thing."

"Well, let's take a short statement now, while it's fresh, then I'll take a formal one later. I really don't know what to ask, at this point.

"She called you, gurgled, and hung up. You came directly up here and found her.

"Was her door open?"

"It was closed, but not locked. I knocked, called, and came in. There she was."

"How long before you called me?"

"Immediately!"

"You stayed right here until I arrived?"

"Yes. Right by the door."

"Thanks. You don't need to stay around for ... did you see anyone at all from when you came here to wait until I arrived?"

She thought a few seconds. "Just Charley Borden. He came home and was going into his apartment just as I came in. Six oh nine. And Mr. and Mrs. Kline went out about five minutes before you got here. Six oh two. That's all."

"Thanks! I'll talk to you again!"

A quick check with Tiny, where Nick learned she'd been dead for no more than two hours nor less than an hour and a half. Nick's watch said seven twenty six. Interesting.

Nick said he'd hang around if Tiny wanted him to, or he'd check out a few things and head for the station. Tiny said he'd transport and seal the room. He didn't need Nick for anything more he knew of.

Nick checked with Frog, who was finished. Frog told Tiny he'd ride back in with Nick. There was something Nick wanted to check, but they'd still beat the van back.

Nick went down to the two cars parked on the outer lot, called in the registration, found the one that had belonged to Jane Warfield and the other to a Charles F. Borden and used his SlimJim to unlock the door to Warfield's. A purse was on the front seat. The keys to the car were inside the damp purse.

"Not very smart to leave a purse in the car, even if it is locked," Frog pointed out.

"The killer left it there when she searched the car. She screwed up fifty ways from sundown on this one."

"You know who killed her? Give!"

"It was perfectly obvious. First, there were those three damp print patterns on the carpet.

"Next, there was a damp area under the window up there. There was a damp spot on the chair by the door. She took too much time."

"Break it down?"

"I pulled into the garage under the building, directly into the parking space for six oh four, yet her car's parked out here, meaning there was a car in it when she got home.

"I didn't know that, of course, but Lucy told me Jane drives her own car, a dark red foreign job. Here, we have a maroon Honda.

"It's raining and there's about an inch of water on this lot, but only two cars and a van. We check the car and find her purse and keys inside. There were three wet print patterns on the hall rug, telling us three people came from outside and got off on six. Jane, Borden, and the killer. If we check, Borden's space will have a car in it. The killer waited in her apartment. She had parked a car in the space for six oh four, meaning that Warfield would park out here.

"The glass in the window is frosted. The killer had it open to watch for Warfield to come in. She parked here and ran in, went up in the elevator and to her room, where she unlocked the door with the key on that ring right there with the car key and what is probably her office key. She put the purse and her plastic rain thing she put over her hair on the chair by the door. She saw that the window was open and closed it. She probably thought she'd left it open, herself.

"She then went to the phone, or maybe started to go into the bedroom. The killer, who was hiding just inside the bedroom door, hit her hard enough to stun her, wrapped the rope around her neck, and killed her.

"The killer then grabbed the purse, ran down here to try to find something in the car, raced back into the garage to move the car that had been in six oh four's space, then back up to call homicide.

"That was the mistake. It took too long. She should have waited. We wouldn't have anything."

"The manager? Why?"

"That's a detail. I don't need a motive for this one. She took too long."

"Oh! I get it! She said she called you when she found the body after getting a phone call and going right up. I heard her telling you that. She called you after six o'clock or you wouldn't have been there. It would have been Jim's case."

"Six oh eight."

"Tiny said no less than an hour and a half and you looked at your wristwatch and got that smug look on your puss. I should've figured it from that. How long had she been dead when you got the call from the manager? What the medallion watch said, five forty?"

"Yup! Now if we find some strange car in Borden's space, it'll tie it – even if I don't need it."

The car was there with the key in the ignition. There were no prints in the car or on the keys, but even the greenest amateur killer knows to wear gloves.

"You gonna arrest her now?".

"Yeah. I don't want to have to spend a whole lot of my time looking for her."

She was packing a bag when Nick and Frog went to pick her up at her apartment. Nick asked where she was going.

"Well, I'm certainly not staying here! There was a murder

committed just upstairs!"

"So? Why should that make you leave? You certainly aren't in any danger from *her* killer."

"How can you be sure of that? What kind of guarantee do I have?"

"You think you're gonna commit suicide?" Frog asked.

"What?! Of course not!"

"Then you ain't in no danger from her killer, are you? You screwed up at least four different ways."

She looked from Frog to Nick and back, started to set her jaw, then deflated.

"Why?" Nick asked her. "You still have the right to remain silent."

"I thought she was planning to expose me for the insurance fraud. I thought that was why she was acting so odd. That she had *me* on that tape. It didn't have anything to do with me. It was just a lot of things she had on ... someone else.

"Will it do me any good to try for acting in a panic?"

"No. You waited by her window, moved the cars around and all that before she got home. There's absolutely no question of it not being premeditated. When it took so long, it was just plain foolish to call us. You should have waited for someone else to find the body."

"I'd left her apartment unlocked. I got out of the car and locked it up, then moved the one parked in Borden's space and remembered her door key was on the car keys. You'd wonder how she got in. I went back up with a spare key to leave by the phone. It would look like she had a spare. I went up and was opening her door and Charley saw me going in. Charley Borden. He opened his door for some reason and saw me, so I called and went on in.

"What could I do? If I didn't think of something he'd tell you I went in! I decided to call nine one one and say that about the phone and gurgle. I guess I knew I'd left too many trails. There wasn't any sense in leaving the key when

Charley would tell you I went in, sooner or later, and I wouldn't have a key. It was going to be so perfect!"

"It never is."

"I'm afraid you'll have to come with us. You can bring a few personal things with you. You'll have to spend at least tonight in jail. I don't know if bail will be allowed, in this case. You'll have to get a lawyer to arrange anything like that.

"You say you found a tape that's about a person other than yourself?"

"I'll get it. Thank you for not being like TV cops."

"If you insist, Nick will call the wagon and put the cuffs on you," Frog said. "It's what he's required to do, but he never pays any attention to that sort of thing. If you act civilized, so will he! My argument is that murder isn't a civilized act."

"You're rather an ass, aren't you? The tape's in here. What will I need?"

"Your purse, a toothbrush, and those kinds of things." They followed back her inside, where she gathered several small things, handed Nick a videocasette, and they drove back to the station where she was being booked. Just as she finished the basic processing Tiny came in to announce he'd found a few things that might help in solving the case, such as the fact Warfield had been struck over the left ear with enough force to cause a severe concussion. She was unconscious, or close to it, when the rope was applied.

"You saw there was no struggle," Tiny said. "I'd say to look at why you weren't called when that woman claimed she'd called."

"She's already booked," Frog reported. "She confessed when Nick confronted her with the evidence."

"I shoulda known! I'm going home," Tiny said, shaking his head tiredly. "She had a business card from Public Union Life Insurance Company in her pocket. It had a phone number on the back and a notation. `Posten claim. Don't pay!'

You might want to check on that. She was a licensed PI who worked on insurance fraud cases." He tossed a plastic bag with the card inside onto Nick's desk.

"Why would I want to check on that?" Nick asked.

"P-U *Life* Insurance Company? That's all. They don't handle any other forms of insurance. She was telling them not to pay? You are a homicide detective. Add it up! Ciao!"

Nick grinned at Frog, sighed heavily, and said to set up the videotape in the Gloom Room (Capt. Paddy James' office) and they'd see what Warfield left for them.

Paddy was head of the violent crimes unit for the county. Sgt. Marsha Blevins, Paddy's aide, actually ran Violent Crimes, most of the time.

Nick called the number on the card, but got a machine that said the offices opened at nine sharp weekdays. He went into Paddy's office. Frog was rewinding the tape, then punched for it to play. It didn't make much sense. First was a woman hanging clothes on a line, then raking a yard. Next was a man who didn't do much of anything except sit by a pool reading a book. Last was another man checking a post office box. #4043. She'd made certain to get that, for some reason.

"I don't get it!" Frog declared.

"Simple. The first one's obvious enough to me," Nick explained. "Consider that Warfield worked for insurance companies."

"Oh, yeah! She's injured *bad*, and can't even *move*! Her whole life's just *ruined*!"

"Warfield could get a very hefty percentage of what they would save if there was a large civil suit settlement or such at stake. The second one doesn't make much sense to me. The third is probably a mail drop for some kind of crook or other. I suppose I'll know more about it in the morning, when I call the company. I'll do the paperwork bit on our case, such as it was, tonight. Maybe there won't be any calls.

"Are you and Dolly coming to Jim's Sunday?"

"Yeah. Dolly wants me to con you into letting us stay at your place in Martinique the first week in April."

"Sure. Nobody's asked for it then." (A supposed drug lord had given Nick a little hideaway on Martinique four years ago. All Nick's friends spent time there in an island paradise anytime they liked – so long as they left the place ready for the next visitor.)

"Great! You're to be my best man. Wednesday, February the twenty eighth! I have to con Lonnie and Serena into letting me have the wedding at their place. Like Pancho and Lonnie. It'll become traditional that the South Station crew gets married at Lonnie's, I suppose."

"They'll dearly love it! Janet and the bunch like planning weddings more than about anything else I can think of!"

Pancho was Pancho DeGulio, the supposed drug lord who gave Nick his cozy hideaway. Nick had become friends of a sort with several very powerful mob syndicate heads. They respected him and kept their "businesses" out of his area. They were all terrified of Pancho, not because of anything he'd done, but because of what he knew. Lonnie Micks was an extraordinarily handsome man Nick met on a case. They had become close friends. Nick had introduced him to Serena Lovell, a stunning redheaded nurse he'd met on two of his cases. They'd fallen totally in love at first sight. Lonnie had always had at least one different woman a day for years, but had settled down with Serena and was "Johnny straight arrow" ever since, though many women were constantly throwing themselves at him, calling him their "Pan."

There wasn't much else to do the rest of the shift. Nick finished the paperwork when Frog left, ran the video, and used the computer to print out still pictures of the three subjects (Dolly, the girl Frog was to marry, was a computer expert, and had set up a program to take a frame and run it on their color printer) to see if the insurance company could identify them, and went home. He'd be in at nine to see what the card and note were about. As Tiny stated, Nick was a homicide cop, and it was a *life* insurance company that wasn't to pay! If he had a case he'd work whenever most convenient. That was Paddy's way of doing things. So far, it had been successful.

Nick sighed, greeted Ellen, and went home to Jan and Cole.

Chapter two

Nick greeted Jim Hill, daytime shift, Paddy and Marsha when he came in the following morning at nine.

"Why are you here?" Paddy asked. "If you have a case, I'll put Ellen on your shift tonight. She wants all the extra experience she can get in investigation. Shirley (Kiser, Graveyard shift head of homicide) has a great job offer in Louisiana she won't be able to turn down. I would never stand in her way. It's a big promotion, so Ellen will take her place when she goes.

"So! Got a case?"

"I don't know yet. That's what I'm here to learn."

"It says here you got a call at six oh eight and booked the woman who committed it at ... ten twenty two – for murder one," Marsha said. "That's pretty good, even for you!"

"We do what we can do. It was one of those things that are so obvious you can't miss them."

"*And* you didn't have anymore calls, yet you have a new case this morning? Spill, honky!"

"There was a note on an insurance company business card that said not to pay on the Posten claim."

"Cute!" Jim said. "And?"

"The murder victim was a PI named Jane Warfield. She worked for insurance companies. The company only deals in life insurance."

"So somebody's supposed to be dead, but isn't? Isn't that the opposite of the job you're so overpaid to be doing, at the moment?" Paddy asked. "Don't we deal mostly with people who aren't supposed to be dead, but are?"

"I want to know why a claim was filed. If there was a body? Maybe it's one of those double indemnity policies or something. An accident that wasn't an accident?

"Chances are I'll make a phone call and drop it. I have to

know. I also have to know what the videotape was all about, but that's probably people who filed claims for phony injuries or disabilities – who don't have the claimed injuries or disabilities."

"Shee! I never know what in the *hell* you're talking about!" Paddy snapped, and stormed back into his office. Marsha grinned.

Nick picked up the desk phone. It took fifteen minutes to find Fred Vincent, who had hired Jane Warfield. The Posten case was about a claim for a two hundred thousand dollar policy, double indemnity, that was filed on when Lyle Norton Posten died in a freak auto accident – or was supposed to have died in one – eleven days ago, on the North Naples bypass road. His sports car had skidded off the road, hit a road sign, hit a tree, and burst into flame.

"Hmm. Then the body was identified how?"

"Bridgework, rather fancy, expensive, the two upper center teeth," Vincent replied. "A Rolex, a money clip, a ruby signet ring."

"You were suspicious for what reason? I need to know why you had decided he wasn't dead."

"Oh, we don't doubt he's dead, really. We do wonder if it was suicide, or if he had a little help when he made his untimely exit. We question the accidental aspect of the case. Miss Warfield was watching the wife."

"I don't...?"

"It seems dear wifey can't explain her whereabouts at the time he died. She was out in her own car.

"A Porsche does *not* catch on fire from that relatively minor kind of accident, as those things go. Several things."

"Mr. Vincent, there's a videotape here I think you may find of some interest. If you'll be free in about half an hour, maybe you could explain some things on it?"

"Yes. You certainly have my curiosity tweaked on this one! I'll be here, or I can come there."

"It's only six blocks or so. I'll bring it over. I'll be there in a few minutes." He hung up.

"I take it you have a case?" Marsha asked.

"I can't say for certain yet, but it sure looks like it. It could be suicide, murder, accidental, or something else. The tape might tell us."

"You can't take a tape from evidence. Have Frog make a copy for you. We have rules! One time in six, we follow them!"

"We don't know if it's evidence or not, yet. We already made a copy. Last night. I don't know if this will lead anywhere." He shook his head, picked up the tape cassette, and headed for the insurance company.

Fred Vincent was a short, paunchy, middle-aged man with a halo of snow white hair around a shiny bald dome. He wore gold-framed glasses he looked over the top of at Nick.

"Fred. You're Lt. Storie?" He offered his hand. Nick shook it and said, "Just Nick. I don't know if this tape is important or not. At the moment, it's a loose end. There are three subjects on it, but I believe one of them will have something to do with the Posten case – or maybe not.

"She had your business card with a note on the back in her handwriting that said not to pay the Posten claim. This is a life insurance company. She was murdered for this video-tape, but it wasn't what the killer thought it would be. The killer evidently thought that Miss Warfield was investigating her."

"She *did* have a note for us not to pay? I find that to be important, if the tape itself isn't. It means we will pursue further investigation.

"It will be a standard size tape. There's a VCR on the office set there. Perhaps I may allow my secretary to view it with us? She has been involved in it ever since the claim was filed, and may spot something I would miss."

Nick nodded and slipped the tape into the VCR while Fred

called his secretary in. He introduced her as Victoria Handy, or simply Viki.

The first subject didn't mean anything to them, but Viki said Jane was working some cases for Florida MedCare Contract Insurance, Inc. who handled various companies' disability, health, and work-related injury policies. Nick wrote the address on his pad.

The second subject got a different reaction! Viki cried, "My god!" just as Fred exclaimed, "Posten!"

"I take it Posten isn't dead? That's him?" Nick asked.

"You take *that* right!" Viki declared. "Where was that taken? Here? Naples?"

"That's the rub! I haven't a clue!"

"Well, he's alive and well!" Fred stated. "We very damned well aren't about to pay Suzanne Posten any four hundred grand! The date and time on that tape is *yesterday afternoon!*

"I want to thank you, Nick. I'll see that you get the forty thousand dollars Miss Warfield would have collected – that is, unless she has a legal partner or something, of course. I *will* most definitely see you're rewarded. This means we save quite a large sum, you see!"

"I'm a cop. It's my job. This means the job is only starting. I'm sure you can understand that."

"Er, I, uh ...?"

"There was a body in that car. That means that someone died.

"Can you stall about the policy, or maybe say nothing?"

"We have nineteen days more, then can say we have discovered new evidence and show it only to a judge," Viki replied. "They'll wonder what we've found, but they won't *know*!"

"I hope I won't need more than that. Do you have any idea what the third person is about or where that PO box is?"

They had no idea.

Nick arranged to get the autopsy and accident reports about

the wreck, and all records the insurance company had were copied quickly by Viki. He took it to his car, then headed across town to MedCare. Viki had called them. They were waiting for him. They agreed the first subject on the tape had filed a claim and taken them to court where she collected sixty thousand dollars for injuries that purportedly left her unable to move her legs or arms more than twenty percent of normal. A professional testifier with a medical license had testified it would take her two years, minimum, before she could hope to work again, and that after some very extensive therapy. The tape would get her on a fraud charge and would put the quack into serious trouble. If they could make a deal with the woman they could probably put the quack in the pen for fraud and perjury.

There was nothing they could tell Nick about the third subject. Nick let them copy a part of the tape concerning the woman and headed for the station. He was just in time to go to lunch with Paddy and Marsha, then went back to Paddy's office to study the tape again, then sat to go through the accident report and autopsy. He started his chart, but didn't have much yet.

On most of his cases Nick made a box chart of the events and people involved. He put each incident in chronological order into the box with the people involved in that event. The murder was in the center box. When he put the victim and another person in that box, the case was solved.

His next order was to find the PO box. He had to have that as part of his case or to eliminate it.

He had several clues. The wall of PO boxes was in a narrow hallway where there were boxes on each side and on the far end. There was a trash can to the left as you entered the hall, and a stamp machine to the right of the end. There was a sign over the stamp machine with an odd darkened area under the postal eagle insignia, as if someone had hidden or blocked out something. It wasn't much, but it would do, he was sure.

He found the PO box at the fourth substation he checked. The postmaster gave him the name of the box renter, LSP Promotions, Inc. The printout of the man using the box wasn't familiar to any of the postal employees.

He'd find everything he needed to know about the postal box. It was probably only a mail drop for a phony company working insurance scams of one sort or another. Maybe a "mail-in your donation to help the starving Scamonians!" type of thing.

It wasn't going to be so easy to find where Posten's little video was made. Probably.

Next, he went to Tiny. Missing persons would work with the coroner's office to try to identify the body from the car from the autopsy reports. The wife had already had the body cremated.

Tiny read over the autopsy reports, shook his head sadly, and said he wished the law was a lot tighter about who could perform autopsies on people who died under such circumstances. The normal hospital doctor didn't look for the same things any criminal investigator would. They would feel they already had positive identification, and that further more thorough proof was unnecessary.

"It's fairly complete, for what it is," Tiny finally said. "I can use it. They *did* retain certain things, such as blood samples for alcohol and drug level certification. The alcohol does seem rather high, if you're interested. He was legally intoxicated."

He flipped slowly through the thin sheaf of papers, went back, frowned, and said, "I would have certainly questioned *that*!"

"What?" Nick asked.

"Severe contusion above and behind the left occipital ridge, three quarters of the way to the ear. There was nothing to cause such damage in a wreck when the victim was wearing his seatbelt. Air bags were deployed?

"How did that survive a fire in the ... here it is. The picture shows his head against the seat headrest. The fire was put out before it had time to ... what a strange angle!

"Good lord, Nick! Didn't a criminologist ever look at these pictures? See the way the seatbelt goes across the shoulder and over here? Let's see you step in the door of a Porsche and have the seatbelt draw like that!"

"What are you saying?"

"Look! The air bag deployed from hitting the sign, and hadn't deflated when the car hit the tree about fifteen feet away! The victim would have been thrown forward – hard into the air bag – and wouldn't even feel the second hit!

"Look at the minor damage to the vehicle, for Christ's sake! The driver would have sworn a blue streak when he got out to see what damage had happened to his expensive toy! The car hit the sign at about forty miles per hour! Certainly no more. It hit the damned tree at less than that speed. The driver wouldn't have been injured at all.

"Next, the body was put in there *after* the accident. It was slid in under the belt with the head turned toward the door – because he was dead or unconscious."

"So. He was murdered, put into the car, and the car set on fire. Either that, or he was put into the car unconscious and was murdered by burning the car with him in it. Either way, it's murder one.

"The cause of death was smoke inhalation?"

"That's what ... I can't find ... anyplace...." Tiny read and mumbled. "I'd say it was *assumed* to be the cause of death from evidence presented. There was no further test made to determine such a minor detail."

"So Posten had somebody ready, unconscious, and ran the car into the sign and tree, got out, put the victim in the car and set it on fire. The wife was there."

"How you figure?" Tiny asked.

"He didn't walk away, and the fire was put out before it did a lot of damage."

"Yes. Somebody followed him out there and drove him away. It occurs something else was left out of the autopsy report. That dental bridge. Did they pull a couple of his teeth and put the thing in his mouth, or did they simply deliver the bridge with the body and the so-called ME didn't bother to look to see if there was even a place for a bridge?"

"Yuck!"

"Very definitely. Yuck! I'll run everything we have on mispers and I'll pick up all the personal effects and samples. Maybe we'll get some kind of break on IDing this one."

"I think we have one strong clue already. The high blood alcohol. He was a drunk they found in a bar somewhere, maybe?"

"Could be. Hmmm. The liver looked mildly sclerotic? It *looked*, for Christ's sake? No examination? The guy was rich, right?"

"I don't know yet. Could be. There was a two hundred grand double indemnity life policy on him, but that's not much for today's standard. We have to see if there's more than ninety percent of this still missing.

"Why?"

"Rich boozers, you don't get too close a check," Tiny said, with a sneer. "Don't want any scandal, you know!"

"Unfortunately, I *do* know. Ciao!"

Nick was fairly sure Tiny would come up with a probable or two on the DB. He'd try to find Posten.

Warfield found him by following Suzanne, the wife.

He went to his office and asked Dolly, their computer whiz, to find what she could about LSP Promotions, Inc., then filed what he had so far. It was a lot – and nothing.

Viki had given him the wife's address. He sighed and informed Marsha he was going to have to try a little stakeout and called his wife to say he was on a case. She'd know what that meant, so far as when he'd be back home was concerned.

The address was out on the Pointe. Money. Number three twenty seven, so merely a few million or so, not the super-rich of numbers one through twelve.

327 Paradise Circle was a reasonably comfortable little 30 room CB bungalow with a red tile roof and a large lot with a deep canal in back. There was a neat 40 foot cabin job at the dock and a shiny new red Corvette in the drive.

A red Corvette and a silver Mercedes.

Nick called in the license plate numbers. The red Corvette belonged to a Wayne Owen Downs. The silver Mercedes was owned by Suzanne Marie Long-Posten. NOW. (No outstanding warrants.)

Nick waited for almost three hours before an attractive if cheap-looking woman came out with a man, kissed him in a rather passionate way, and he turned to get into the fancy Corvette. He was the one from the post office.

Nick called in to report that the third subject on the tape was a Wayne Owen Downs. He wanted the address from the license plates.

3712 Downwind Drive, Apt. 316. Greengate Estates.

Nick didn't know whether to follow Wayne Downs now or to stay to watch Suzanne Posten. He opted for the latter. She didn't leave the house until a short while after 10:00. Nick fell in behind and followed at about a block back. There was enough normal traffic to make him inconspicuous as she drove north to Interlock Road, then out Airport Road a ways. She turned off on Juanita Lane, went to the end and right on W. Hutton Place. She pulled into the drive of 434, parked in the garage (for which she had a radio-control) and the door closed. Nick parked about halfway down the block and strolled casually past and around the corner. He could then look directly across the back yard of the house at 432. There was a pool enclosure. The whole area was very well-lit, so details stood out well. A stroll on around the block let him see into a corner of the screened enclosure through the property behind. He could see the table in the video.

So. Should he just get it over with?

Definitely not yet! He had very little except insurance fraud. He had to know more about how Downs fit into whatever was going on. So long as Posten didn't suspect he'd been found, he'd stay put.

Nick strolled back to his car and sat a moment, thinking of as many angles as he could. This was definitely not what it looked like – or it was. How you looked had much to do with what you saw. If it weren't for Downs, this would be easy to figure. With him in it, it didn't figure at all. He could merely be a dirty little side affair Suzanne was having, but the fact Warfield took a video of him at that PO box screamed that he was far more than he seemed.

Whatever, Nick was worn out, and it was getting close to the time he went off shift, normally. He'd just finished a double, and was tired. Dolly would have whatever was known about Downs for him in the morning – no. She would have what that company was about. That would, hopefully, tell him what Downs was about, and how he figured into the mess.

Never a dull moment!

"Did you get anything for me on LSP Inc.?" Nick asked, as he poured himself a cup of coffee and brought one to Dolly.

"It's a tax writeoff. It supposedly produces a few TV commercials and runs a telephone solicitation scam. LSP is owned by Lyle and Suzanne Posten and a man by the name of Wayne Downs. Downs is CEO, and owns half.

"Seeing this has something to do with your case, I looked up the original partnership agreement. It's a rights of survivor thing. Downs now owns sixty seven percent and Suzanne Posten owns the rest. Any help?"

"It tells me that something smells of rotten fish a lot closer than Denmark! Now I have to wonder exactly what the hell this crap is about! I didn't figure anything even close! Is this Downs and Suzanne, Downs and Posten, Downs alone, Suzanne and Posten, Suzanne alone, or Posten alone? All of them?

"I'm going backwards on this one. All I've got is a cremated dead body with an incomplete autopsy who was identified as being Posten."

"You do get the interesting cases. I think there's a lot I don't know and a lot I don't want to know.

"Call Tiny. Frog has a note on the comp."

Nick saw the flashing little box that said, "Have Nick call Tiny." He sighed heavily and went to his desk phone to punch for forensics. Tiny came on and said he had a probable on the DB. A homeless alcoholic who did odd jobs over near Immokalee and who hung around a pub called Pete's Palace. Nick would check that out to give him time to think over the case. He was directed to check on someone they called "Boats."

Pete's was a sort of rundown beer and wine bar that served cold sandwiches and pizzas with the beer. It catered to the low-paid workers in the poorest section. Pete was Al Blandinghouse, who bought the place for next to nothing two years ago – and that's what it was worth. Next to nothing.

"It's a real bitch!" Al confided. "You got to run tabs for when they get paid, then half of them never come around again.

"I mean, they'll come in regular for a couple months, you think they won't stiff you, because where else they gonna get booze? Then they stiff you and move to Homestead or some- where and you got a tab of maybe fifty or a hunnert. It ain't really that much, but I got bunches of 'em!

"Just what you wanna hear, right?"

"I don't think I'd give an alky credit."

"You don't, and nobody comes in!"

"What about Boats? He run a tab?"

"Yeah. He gets it to maybe twenny bucks'n works for a day sos he can pay up. Genius, in some ways, just can't fight the booze. Drinks cheap wine. His tab's about six bucks, right now. I ain't seen 'im in ten, twelve days, but he'll be back.

"Wait a minute! You're a homicide cop askin' about 'im, and I know he ain't killed anybody! He ain't comin' back?"

"That's a very distinct possibility. I'll need as close a description as you can give. I need to know what his real name is."

"He's about my height. Five eleven. Maybe just a little bit thinner. I weigh in a hunnert ninety five, he'd go about maybe a hunnert seventy. Black hair. Dark eyes. Sometimes he shaved – sometimes not.

"I ain't got any idea what his name is. A guy knew him in Nola called him 'Hawk' once, but that's all I'd ever heard but 'Boats'. He sleeps in those old boats in back of the junk-yard's where that tag comes from. Bick says he keeps the others from ripping him off at night, he can stay back there. Even has this tiny kerosene stove he cooks stuff on. Makes really good stew out of rabbits or that kind of stuff.

"He's got a real good talkin' voice, you know? Like one'a them radio disc jockeys. Smooth. I think he makes voice commercials or something, sometimes. I cashed a check once from some ad agency. Biggest one he ever brought in. Over a hunert bucks!"

"How were his teeth?"

"Teeth? They were all his, I guess. Maybe one or two missing ... he had a fight once and got one knocked out, I think. I don't remember. I think he had a phony tooth he'd take out now and again. You could ask Cage."

"Cage?"

"He's the guy from Nola. Cajun. Everbody calls him Cage, or Mardi, for Mardi Gras. He always talks about Mardi Gras. He'll be in tonight. Gets paid. He's one who pays his tab ever week, sure as sundown. Works two days for the farms and pays his tab with one day and buys stuff he needs, like food, with one day. Drinks a lot, and can get mean and want to fight, but he's no alky, you know? He's living just like he wants to live."

"What time will he come in?"

"Five, five thirty. He'll pay his tab and have a big pitcher and cheese pizza."

"Thanks, I'll come back then."

"Do us both a favor?"

"What?"

"Don't, like announce that you're no cop?" He grinned.

"You got it, but they'll know. I won't deny it," Nick returned the grin.

"You're probably big enough to take care of yourself, but I'm not in it!"

"Fair enough!"

Chapter three

There were a couple of older cars and four trucks at the bar when Nick parked the Trans Am at five thirty. Some teenage kids were hanging around out front and one gave him a sneering look, then raised an eyebrow at the Trans Am.

Nick returned the sneer. "You could mess with someone like me and never be heard of again. Comprende?"

There was no malice in it. The boy grinned and said, "Frio, hombre! No hay problema!"

"Es cierto!" Nick agreed, and went inside. They wouldn't mess with his car.

"Cage here?" he asked, as he went to the bar to order a short beer.

"Who wants to know?" the bartender asked, pouring the draft with far too much head. Nick took the dollar bill he'd dropped back off of the counter. The bartender grinned, scraped the head, and added some beer. Nick paid for the beer and said, "Al told me I'd probably find him here tonight. Could be a friend of his died."

"Oh. He said," the bartender replied, pointing to a large, dark man sitting in a booth in back, eating a pizza.

Nick nodded and went back to ask, "Cage?"

"Yeah."

"I'm Nick. I have to ask you a few questions. I think Boats is dead."

"Al done said. You the cop we're not supposed to know is a cop?" He looked amused.

"That was Al's suggestion, not mine." Nick grinned.

"He said."

"Do you know what Boats' real name was?"

"We called him Hawk in the bayou. Don't know his given name. Had a good education. Alky got to him when a woman worked him over. Served some time in N'Orlins. They'll have it."

"Serious trouble?"

"D and D. Affray. DUI. That kind of stuff."

"He worked in radio. Ads? Good voice?" Cage was NOT about to volunteer anything, but he would answer a direct question.

"Said. And phone scams. Sang some, but a good talkin' voice ain't necessarily a good singin' voice. Too smooth. Maybe big band crooner crap."

"Know who he did ads for here?"

"Didn't. Phone scam crap. Recorded. Called a buncha old widows through a computer and his voice said they were selected from a list of special people to send him money for phony charities or something. He said."

"Who?"

"Lisp something ink. He said. Friend of the owner. Did talk twice a month."

"This will sound strange, but we have to know," Nick said, choosing his words very carefully. "What do you know about his teeth?"

"He still had most of 'em except for two in the front. Top center. There was a guy didn't like his face, he didn't like the guy's face, so they changed 'em for each other."

"Wore a bridge?"

"Yeah. Get drunk and take it out. Real great way to pick up broads – except he didn't like broads. He'd gross 'em out and they'd leave him alone. Wasn't queer. Just that one woman screwed him up bad. Wasn't gonna let it ever happen again."

"Nick couldn't think of anything else at the moment. "Thanks."

"Like to fight?"

"No. I see 'way too many messy results."

"It'd give me status to kick a cop's ass."

"If you could. What about when the cop kicks yours? What happens to your status then?"

He laughed. "Nothing! I had the guts to try! It's no-lose for me!"

"So long as I didn't decide to blow your head off when you got me pissed. That would be no-lose for me! I'm a cop! I did what cops do!"

"Ha! Don't make me like you! *That* would hurt my status!"

"Nah. I'm a likeable kinda guy."

"Yeah, I guess so. If somebody corked Boats, you gonna do anything about it?"

"Well, other than try to see them strapped in the chair and barbecued, probably not much."

"Gonna try too hard?" he asked, leaning back and giving Nick his amused look.

"As hard as with anybody else. It's what I do."

Cage saluted him with his beer. Nick drained his own glass, stood, nodded, and left.

Nobody had messed with his car.

Okay. Lisp something ink would about have to be LSP Promotions Inc. He could probably find a lot more from New Orleans about Boats. He didn't doubt it was his body in the burnt car. Boats was a friend of the owner of LSP. He had the same type two-tooth bridge upper center as Posten. He was missing – and Posten was alive and well.

How long ago had this thing been planned? Downs had a body ready to become the body for how long?

Something else occurred to Nick. It was based on the type of person who would do this kind of thing: Did LSP carry a large insurance policy on Posten?

Nick called the insurance company to be told Viki was working on posting the new stats and interdepartmental schedule. She would be there until nine o'clock.

Nick went to the company and asked Viki if there was a way to trace if there were other policies in force on Posten when he supposedly died.

"I can do a cross-ref. Give me about ten minutes and I'll see what the comps turn up, but we did an automatic trace on named insureds when we first got suspicious."

She worked at her computer terminal for a few minutes, then grinned at Nick. "Bingo! It didn't show on first scan because the policy wasn't specifically in his name. It's in a company name, and pays if any of the owners die. Two million each. I'll notify the company not to pay."

"LSP Promotions, Inc.?"

"No. Post Productions, of Atlanta."

"Check on LSP Productions. See if they also have a policy. Can you find others?"

"Mmm-hmm! LSP Promotions? I'll see if any company has a ... whew!"

"Whew?"

"Five million bucks. Any holding officer. Not filed."

"Can you find any others? I mean that aren't filed. *Yet*!"

"Only if we find company names. I imagine there will be several, don't you?"

"It's a distinct possibility."

"Have you found who the body in the car was yet?"

"Yes, and no. We know he was known as 'Boats' here and as 'Hawk' in New Orleans. We'll get a complete on him before the day's over.

"It looks like he was found, cultivated, and kept ready for this scheme for quite some time. If I ever had *any* case where I could definitely prove premeditation, this is it! I'll let you know when we have anything else."

They talked a few minutes more, then Nick headed back to the office. Dolly wasn't there that late, so Nick called at Frog's apartment to ask her how to use the comp interchange to get the information from New Orleans. She said she'd come over and run it for him right quick. Frog's was directly across the alley from forensics, which was one block away. They were there in ten minutes.

Ten minutes later Nick went to the forensics lab to pick up the ME's fingerprint records, then Dolly faxed them to New Orleans. The police had pulled the files on everyone there who had used an alias of "Hawk" that they had any records on. It took about three minutes for the match to come back.

Donald Jerome Mathews, Jr. Born on August 24, 1947. Baton D'Or, Louisiana. Married Janine Laverne LaBelle, May 1974, two male offspring ... M degree in horticulture LSU, divorced June 17, 1982. Bitter. Grnds:Infidelity (multiple) against wife. Husband granted full custody. Chld Sprt by trust. Both children residing with paternal grand-parents.

There were several petty misdemeanor charges for which he was prosecuted and for which he served short sentences.

"Very typical and sad," Dolly remarked.

"He left a trust fund to support his kids? How do I find what's in that?"

Dolly grinned and worked for a few minutes on her comp. She typed in information from the police reports and from the death certificate for Posten, then had to explain it wasn't Posten, but Donald Jerome "Hawk" Mathews who had died. Mistaken ID from the first. That information was to be treated as sealed and confidential, as it was evidence in a murder investigation.

"The fund has a base principle of two hundred fifty thousand dollars, which remains until the boys' twentieth birthdays when they receive the principle," Dolly read. "Interest is paid directly to the D. J. Mathews in Baton D'Or on a fixed monthly schedule. Does that change anything?"

"It surprises me, but doesn't change anything. He met his financial responsibilities for his family before he became a drunk. I have to respect that!"

The rest of the shift was spent on a hit-and-run on airport road. A woman was run down with a rusty old brown Ford pickup truck as she crossed at a corner. The truck came from her rear, turned, there she was. If the driver had stopped, it wasn't very likely he would have even been charged. Overgrown shrubbery on the corner made it almost impossible to see her.

The description of the truck meant they'd find it in no more than ten or twelve hours. There was probably a reason he didn't stop. It would come out. The routine manner of these types of investigations did give Nick a respite from what was becoming a more and more puzzling case. He still didn't know who to charge with what.

"Uh, officer?" a woman said timidly, as the coroner's wagon was driving off and Nick was heading for his car.

"Yes?"

"I tried to tell that highway patrol cop I know which truck hit Alice, but he kept saying he'd get right back to me, then he just drove off!"

"You do? Which one?"

"The tall one. White, not the black one."

"You lost me. Which truck was it?"

"Oh. I thought you meant which cop. It's an old red truck that comes to the Givins' place, number seven seventy six ten, all the time. That's the place two blocks down. Big Australian pine tree in the yard and that white boat. I think they play cards and maybe go fishing and all that kind of thing."

"I'll check it out while I'm here, anyway. Thanks. I won't mention where I got the word. No sense in causing friction among neighbors."

She shrugged. "You wouldn't. There's already plenty of that here! Nobody likes anybody!"

"Too bad."

"Not really." She turned and walked away.

Nick grinned, got in his car, and drove to the house, where a Ralph Donner said he didn't know anybody in a truck like that.

"You know what aiding and abetting a felon is? All I have to do is find two people who saw that truck here and you're gone for three to five.

"What? He drunk or something?"

Ralph sighed. "I don't know. He could be, but it's a little too early for that. Gordon Miller. He don't have any insurance or a license. He didn't see her, turned in, and hit her, then he panicked.

"I've been tryin' to get that crap cut for two years. Had to happen, sooner or later.

"What'll they do to him?"

"It will depend on a couple of things. Why no license or insurance?"

"He couldn't afford insurance, so couldn't get renewal on his license. The truck has an expired on it."

"No moving violations?"

"Not that I know of. He was extra careful. Couldn't afford to get stopped."

"He'll probably get fined. He can get off from leaving the scene by claiming he panicked because of no license. I agree there was little likelihood he saw her. It's in the report.

"No insurance is bad news. He could get the rest of his life attached if she has any family who'll pursue it.

"I'm going back to the station. If he comes in and owns up, it'll look a lot better for him. South Station."

"He hit Alice Fordyce?"

"Yes."

"She's got nobody. She's probably dead drunk, herself. She usually was."

"If she had high blood alcohol, he'll get off a lot easier. It's possible she wasn't even aware of her surroundings and stepped out in front of him. He should have stopped. He had it all in his favor until he ran."

"I'll try to get him to come in. He would anyhow, I guess. He couldn't live with it."

Nick nodded, said goodbye, and headed back to the station. Gordon Miller came in half an hour later. Nick took a short statement and called the state's attorney.

"You've talked to him about it, Nick," Ray Graham, the prosecutor, said tiredly. "Do I have to come down there?"

"You have to sign the charges is all. You can do that tomorrow, but he'll have to stay in jail overnight, if you do."

"And?"

"He's not going to run."

"Okay. Tell him he can go home on his own recognizance. He's to leave the truck there. You take full responsibility. We'll talk tomorrow morning. He can plea and I'll go easy for this, but he's going to receive a pretty stiff fine."

"You can work it out. Good night." He hung up and told Gordon he'd drop him off on his way home. He was to go to the courthouse at nine in the morning and talk to Ray Graham.

"I'm sticking my neck 'way out. Don't keep acting this stupid. Be there, and work it out. You have to start taking some responsibility. You won't get time, and will be given time to pay the fine if you cooperate and don't miss any appointments."

"You're the most decent cop I've ever come across!" Gordon said. "I guarantee I'll be there."

Ellen came on half an hour later. Nick dropped Gordon at his house and went home to his wife.

"Well?" Paddy greeted. "Anything new?"

"We know who the DB is," Nick answered. "We know Downs was preparing this for some time. I have to find out just how long. It seems there are other companies who are filing a policy claim or two on good friend Posten. Multimillion dollar claims."

"It's about time we picked him up and put an end to this, isn't it? What don't we know?"

"More than we do. It's not even a little bit clear what's really going on. If we pick him up, will he throw Suzanne and Downs to us or keep them out of it? We don't get them if he clams."

"Really? After we can show this Downs character had the person who supplied the body setup for who knows how long?" Marsha asked. "Come *on*!"

"How do we prove that?"

"By putting your source on the stand," Paddy replied.

"Yeah, right, and sure! Cage will really be a dream witness!"

"He's lying?" Marsha asked.

"No."

"He's not a very credible witness," Paddy agreed. "Not that he'd lie, but because the jury won't believe him if some clever smartass lawyer gets up there and makes him lose his temper.

"Nick will figure something. He always does. As for us, I have to go to a stupid luncheon with a bunch of cheap politicians – that you set up!

"So guess what, Sgt. Blevins! You set that crap up, and you're going with me!"

"Hey! I ain't got the time to go to any stupid political PR luncheon waste of time! It's part of *your* job description, not *mine*!"

"Hah-ah! *You* keep telling those bighead bad muckety-mucks I'll be there, so from now on *you* go with me to take notes! Got it?"

"I think there won't be many more of them, will there? I'd better see if I can find a starting place here in the middle of this muddle."

Marsha and Paddy soon went out. Marsha was whining about how sneaky he was getting, while Paddy smiled broadly and told her it was about time she learned what the political ass-kissing was like, seeing as how she was so interested in putting *him* into those situations.

Nick grinned at Jim Hill. Jim said it was just about time Paddy put her in her place. She was beginning to use the silly political meetings to get Paddy out of the office.

"She runs the place anyway. It keeps him from getting underfoot all the time."

"That would be fine with Paddy, but he gets the blame whenever she screws up. She's getting to where she feels a bit too powerful."

"So what's it really about? The promotions list?"

"Yeah. It's mostly an act to convince them about something."

"I thought Marsha liked where she is?"

Jim tossed the latest promotions list to Nick. Marsha was up for a promotion. Nick thought a minute, and grinned. "I see. She does *not* want that promotion!"

"Right! It would put her right in line to head special security."

"PR and interference for that bunch of cruds at city hall she hates with a passion!" Nick laughed. "They hate her as much. They'll grab onto any opportunity to refuse her that raise in grade. Paddy'll get pissed and give her a ... he would never do that!

"I'll be damned! Paddy's being manipulated into doing exactly what she wants!"

"Paddy's smarter than that. He's playing the game the way she wants for his own reasons. She goes to those political things, she'll manage to aggravate the crummy politicians who have to sign off on her promotion. They'll get POed and refuse, doing exactly what Paddy *and* Marsh want. On top of it, Marsh won't schedule anymore of those things than she's forced to. Those hacks are *not* as smart as either of our two! I mean, really! Can you picture Paddy being manipulated by *anybody*? Gimme a break!"

Nick laid out his case, filled in his box chart, then sat back to think. He knew exactly what had happened, to this point, but not why. Not really.

What was Posten planning to do with the payoffs from the insurance scams? He damned well couldn't stay in the south. Not with policies in several states.

He planned to leave the USA, most probably. That would have to be prevented.

Something else occurred to Nick then: It was *Downs* who had Hawk set up to supply a body for quite some time, *not* Posten! Downs was apparently having an affair with the lovely Suzanne – so was *he* behind it or was *she*?

Nick wanted to know exactly how smart Posten was. How smart was Downs? How smart was Suzanne?

Well, he could easily find out about Downs and Suzanne. He picked up his notes, put them and his chart in his desk drawer, and headed for LSP Promotions, Inc.

"Mr. Downs, Det. Lt. Storie." The efficiently severe private secretary announced. Nick stepped into the plush office as she stepped out and closed the door.

"Yes, Lt. Storie?" Downs said, waving to a chair that was a bit lower that his own. Nick went to the desk to place a copy of the policy on Posten in front of Downs, then sat in the chair on that side of the desk. A higher chair.

"Why haven't you filed on that?" Nick asked.

Downs read it over as if it was something he'd never seen and looked at Nick in as innocent a way as he could muster to say, "I didn't know about it, or I certainly would have!"

"You didn't know about it? Yet your signature is right there next to Posten's and his wife's? You also signed the checks that were paid for the policy every March."

"I sign fifty checks every day. I almost never actually look at them. I signed hundreds of things when we were starting the business."

"I see. You just hope someone doesn't slip a check into the

batch that will break the place. I take it you also don't know that you filed for the business in Atlanta, either? That two million policy will come as a huge surprise to you?"

"That one, I knew. That little business is run very differently than this one. I'm here. That one is run by a couple of flunkies.

"What's this about?"

"We have solid reason to believe Posten is alive and well and living in the Bahamas. That brings homicide into it in a very big way."

"It brings homicide into it if Posten *isn't* dead? How droll!" Downs sneered. "Wouldn't it tend to work the other way around?"

"Only if you overlook minor details."

"Oh? Such as?" he asked, as condescendingly as he could manage.

"There *was* a body in that car, now wasn't there?" Nick was even more condescending.

Chapter four

Suzanne Posten was next. Nick pulled into the winding drive and parked across from the Mercedes. He went to the door, rang the bell, and a maid in an attractive starched blue uniform answered.

"Lt. Nick Storie," Nick said. "I wish to speak with Suzanne Posten about the death of her husband."

"Mrs. Posten isn't seeing anyone."

"Inform her that I have to ask her a few pertinent questions about the *supposed* death of her husband."

"Mrs. Posten isn't seeing anyone."

"I see. Very well. Then tell her I'll send an officer with an arrest warrant. I merely wished to spare her the embarrassment of having to be transported to the station in the cage, undergoing a search, and being held in a cell until the judge has time to see her to order her to answer. You might also tell her to call a lawyer and have him waiting. She's damned well going to need one.

"Good day!"

He made it to his car and was getting in when the maid came to call to him that Mrs. Posten would speak with him.

"Just tell her I was doing her a favor coming here. I'm not playing games. She can enjoy a free ride to the station and can answer all the questions with a legal stenographer and her lawyer present. Tell her I'm with homicide, and we think her husband is alive and well."

He started his car and put it in gear. Suzanne ran out to tell him the girl had misunderstood. She merely didn't want to be bothered with "...all those greedy people trying to get their hands on the money."

"Uh-huh. And Downs didn't call you and tell you I would be coming.

"Mrs. Posten, I told the girl I wasn't here to play a silly

game. You'd better wake up! If, as we're beginning to suspect, your husband is still alive, it's not a simple case of insurance fraud where you'll spend a few months in some luxury pen and get away with a few million dollars for the trouble."

"I don't know what you're talking about! My husband is dead! If there was some kind of insurance fraud, it doesn't have anything to do with *me*!

"What do you mean it's something else? If he's still alive, it's *him* who's doing it, not *me*"

"Mrs. Posten, we're talking about murder here. Like it or not, that's more serious than any life insurance fraud charge."

"But ... what are you talking about? If he's not dead, what does murder have to do with anything?"

"You had a body cremated. *Somebody's* dead! If your husband's alive, we have to account for that body, and we have to explain how it ended up in your husband's Porsche – after which *you* identified it as being your husband. *Dead* in your husband's Porsche, Mrs. Posten.

"You've never told us where you were during the time that your husband's car ended up burning with a dead body in the driver's seat. Care to comment?"

"I told them I was shopping at the Bell Tower In Ft. Myers!" She looked scared.

"Fine! They print the date and time on the receipts. That should be easy enough to prove."

"I didn't buy anything! I just shopped! I don't buy anything, half the time. I just *shop*!"

"Did you see or speak to anyone who might remember you being there?"

"No! I don't know anyone in Ft. Myers!"

"Did you buy gas for your car?"

"No."

"Not much of an alibi, is it?"

"I didn't know I'd be needing one, or I would have a

hundred receipts and witnesses! I don't think Lyle's alive. The man at the hospital, Dr. Akins, said that the identification was really definite. The chance of anybody else having a bridge like his was so close to zero it wasn't even worth considering!" She seemed to be getting more confident.

"Thousands of people wear bridges."

"*Not* like Lyle's! His was a very good, very expensive one that was positively the one from Lyle Posten's body in the car!"

"You know one little fact about bridges?"

"What?"

"They come out. We *will* be in touch again, Mrs. Posten. Have a nice day!" He drove off. She stood in the drive, staring after him. Nick drove out the gate, then parked not far along the road to wait for more than an hour, but she didn't leave. He went to the station, checked his messages, thought for a few minutes, and headed for South General Hospital.

Dr. John James Akins was the senior pathologist. Yes, he did all autopsies when there was any likelihood of question. Yes, he was on premises at the moment – and no, Lt. Storie could not have a moment of his time. He was in the POR, working. He would be free in an hour or so, that assuming no unforeseen complications arose.

Nick detected some kind of tension while asking about Akins. He used his most winning smile (which had less than zero effect on the super-efficient Personal Administrative Asst. P. B. Browning) and remarked, "Dr. Akins seems to cater a bit to the wealthy, I hear." A nurse filing folders near the counter grinned at him and rolled her eyes.

"I'm sure I don't care to listen to gossip!" she retorted, acidly. "All doctors must, as you say, cater to the wealthy, as that's where the grants and donations come from that keep this and most other facilities operating.

"If that is all? I will page you as soon as the doctor is free to speak with you."

Nick nodded shortly, and left the counter. He decided to go to the cafeteria for a hot cup or two of coffee while he waited. A few minutes later the nurse from the pathology office came to smile down at him. He offered her a seat at the cramped little table for two, standing as she took her seat.

"How truly quaint!" she exclaimed, with an impish grin. "An actual gentleman! These doctors and interns ... well!

"I can assume you were sufficiently impressed by Nurse Pinch Butt Browning, queen of cold efficiency, protector of the realm, and all that?"

"Pinch Butt?" Nick asked, with a quick grin.

"Pinched so tight she has to use the jaws of life to take a crap! The initials stand for Portia Berenice, but we call her Miss Browning, MA'AM.

"She's had a crush on Akins for years. Anybody else was after him, we'd never understand it. Her, it figures.

"You asked her about the hoity-toits. He kisses their asses with fervor approaching gusto.

"What's up?"

"It seems likely he identified a dead body that even a cop on a beat could tell wasn't who he said it was. We wonder why."

"Akins? Somebody probably told him the body looked like a person they met once ten years ago, and that's what the tag said was possibly the name, so it must be. He once identified a Jane Doe as being Beverly Smythe, because there was a "B" embroidered on a lace handkerchief stuffed into her bra, she was about the height and weight on the MP report, and she had shortish sandy hair, brown eyes, and two irregular teeth. She was approximately thirty two years old and had a tobacco habit."

"And?"

"He didn't bother to look at the little box labeled "Sex" on the MP form. Beverly Smythe was a man from England. The DB was a woman from, it turned out, Mississippi."

"Details! Details!" Nick laughed. "Could he be bought?"

"Not for money, but he can be conned. I've seen him report positive identification by a close relative on more than one occasion when there wasn't any such thing. A wife or sister can come in with the wailing faints, say she just *couldn't* face this ghoulish horror, and he'd say the person was this high and so heavy and had such and such colored hair and eyes, the poor distraught thing says it just *has* to be daddy or mommy or hubby or whatever and he lets them sign the ID form. If you could be sure he'd get the ME job, you could really work some scams on insurance companies with him! Have some woman come in crying and faint, say ... oh! You're a cop! Did I just put my foot in it and get fired without a hint of recommendation?"

"Beg pardon?" Nick answered, taking a small sip of the truly terrible coffee. "I was thinking about this insurance fraud case I'm on and didn't hear a word you might have said."

"You're wearing a wedding ring, but you're very sexy, human, and attractive. You're a gentleman, while also being a man. With my regular luck you don't fool around!"

"Your luck's sure consistent!" Nick laughed again. "I'm Nick Storie."

"Leanne. Friends call me Lee."

"What does Pinch Butt call you?"

"*Miss* or *nurse* Upton!" She laughed. "Turn about's fair play – and you're a lot of fun, Nick. I like you!"

"Lt. Storie, report to pathology! Stat! Lt. Storie, report to pathology!" came over the PA.

"You heard her! Report! Immediately! Hup! Hup!" Nick grinned, stood, saluted, and marched in fine tin soldier military fashion out of the cafeteria.

Dr. Akins was short, fat, affable, in a phony sort of way,

and left no least nagging question that he was overworked, tired, and harried to a truly unbelievable degree. P. B. Browning hovered over him, giving him hot coffee and sweet rolls and generally mothering to him. Nick was very pointedly *not* offered coffee and rolls. She finally left his office and he asked Nick what was the problem?

"You did an autopsy on a Lyle Norton Posten, who died in a burning car," Nick said. "It was on August six."

"Hmm. Let me get the file. I don't recall exactly ...." He punched the intercom and went on, "Miss Browning, please bring me the AD report on a Lyle Norton, August six of this year?"

"Lyle Norton Posten." Nick corrected.

She marched in through the door with it almost immediately. That was taking efficiency to an extreme. Nick cocked his head toward the side and raised an eyebrow at her.

"We had a question asked by Dr. Menthorne. County. I had the report ready for your review. Lt. Storie forgot to mention Dr. Menthorne sent him for the information, I take it."

"No, I had no idea Tiny had called. I should have known he would. He isn't very tolerant of certain things." Nick turned back toward Akins, making it very plain Browning was dismissed. She colored and stamped out.

"Uh-oh?" Akins said.

"Can you take me through the ID process used on this case?"

"It seems rather mundane and simple," Akins sat at his desk to read the report. "What's the problem?"

"Other than the fact the body was that of a man named Donald Jerome Mathews, and there are some tens of millions of dollars in fraudulent insurance claims in the name of Lyle N. Posten, nothing of much importance."

"Hmm?" Akins replied, reading the report over again quickly, and turning to pull a file from the cluttered shelf behind him. He went through the file and replied, "Hmm. A woman claiming to be his wife, Suzanne Poston – and producing positive identification proving she was, in truth, his wife, viewed the body, and said she was quite sure it was her husband. We had the man's wristwatch, a money clip, the fact it was his automobile, and a rather fancy ... I remember now! Yes! He had a very unusual dental piece. There was simply and absolutely no question whatever that it was the subject's dental work, Lt. Storie."

"You removed the bridge from the corpse?"

"From the mouth, yes."

"It was in place?"

"It was jarred loose, but was still partially in place, Lt. Storie," he said, condescendingly. "No one knocked out two teeth and placed the thing. The tooth removal was quite old, and the gums were tempered from such use."

"But the bridge you removed was not the one that had been worn there for a number of years. Boats wore a two-tooth bridge in the same location for some years. He would show the tempering of the jaw and gums. The bridge you removed from the body wouldn't have fit properly, had you tried to place it.

"You followed procedure properly here. This was a murder. It was planned for a very long time. We believe Posten is alive and well, and possibly living in the Bahamas, or some-place such. He now intends having some millions of dollars in insurance claims paid to his wife and businesses, after which he will suddenly reappear as another person. He'll marry his poor dear grieving widow and live happily and luxuriously ever after.

"Suzanne did view the corpse directly? She identified it as being her husband?"

"Er, well, she looked quickly and, er, got sick, but she did say it was definitely and positively her husband. She was quite sure."

"Positively, or quite sure?"

"Well, er, quite sure, actually. We had what we thought was positive identification, so we didn't insist, er, that is...."

"I see. She was upset. She could possibly have been mistaken in her identification?"

"Yes! Exactly! Quite distraught, as you can well imagine! The body was severely burned in some areas."

"Not a very pretty thought – and a far less pleasant sight."

"Exactly! These women can go all to pieces over such things, you know. Very uncomfortable. Very uncomfortable indeed! For everyone concerned!"

"So I hear. Thank you. We'll have to try to unravel who's involved and who isn't in these kinds of things. Do *not* tell *anyone* what was discussed here."

"Oh, you can count on me! I find this to be most distressing. We want, more than anyone, for it to be resolved! And rapidly!"

Nick nodded, stood, and left, thinking, *Because you could end up answering some uncomfortable questions yourself!*

Nick went back to the station and began piecing odd things together. Things were beginning to fit, but he wasn't really any closer to finding the answer to the basic question of who was involved, and exactly how.

Posten, himself, without any doubt whatever.

Downs was definitely involved, but in what way? He had the body ready and waiting. He was as guilty as Posten, in every legal sense. He couldn't claim he didn't mean to kill Mathews. Those two were solid. The question now was Suzanne. She was a big part of it, but of the insurance scam or the murder? Or both? Was the whole thing her plan? Downs'? Posten's?

Well, the fraud wasn't questionable. She knew he was alive and was seeing him. She was that deep into it.

Was that enough?

It wasn't very likely any of them were going anywhere

soon, except for Posten, himself. They might have plans to get him away until the case was forgotten, but Nick had mentioned to everyone with any connection with him that the cops thought he was in the Bahamas – which would make it safest to keep him right where he was.

That was the theory, anyhow.

Nick filled in his box chart. It was fairly complete for the time of the murder until now. There was very little in the boxes before the murder, only such details as Downs somehow finding Mathews and cultivating him. There was a disturbing question with this kind of thing that was always there: Was this their first time?

Nick was now going to be looking into the pasts of his major players in this game!

"Dolly, can you start a tracing of Wayne Owen Downs, thirty seven twelve Downwind Drive, Lyle Norton Posten and wife Suzanne Marie Long-Posten of three twenty seven Paradise Circle, the Pointe?" Nick asked. "I'll need everything there is to know about them from the womb to now."

"Yup! That's what I'm here for! Learning a thing or two about this bunch?"

"I have hundreds of odd little facts, but they don't begin to add up yet. It's an insurance scam that depends on murder, but is this the first? It seems very practiced. Do you know what I mean?"

"I think so. Tiny said the blood had a very high alcohol content, but it also had some other things that could use explaining."

"Such as?"

"Almost no unprocessed sugars."

"Hmm. So he was given insulin?"

"Enough to put him into a coma!"

"It's a test that wouldn't normally be run on a burn victim. A mickey would show up from the regular alcohol scan, but sugar tests wouldn't be made. See what I mean? About how practiced it seems?"

"They studied it very carefully. It'll take a couple of hours to trace these three. I have the full cooperation of the two insurance companies you saved all that money. They'll help with a lot of information.

"Paddy wants to talk to you. Marsh is in his office. They've got their heads together over something."

Nick nodded, and went into Paddy's office. He gave Paddy a report on what he'd discovered so far.

"You have enough for a probable warrant on both Posten and Downs now," Paddy argued. "Why not tag their asses and let them put the Mrs. in the middle of it?"

"Because this might not be their first time. Dolly's tracing. What if they got the original money to start their cute little scam companies by killing someone else? This seems a bit too well-planned, Paddy. They knew about way too many details. If Warfield hadn't put that note on the card, they would've gotten away with it."

"If she hadn't written that note and if anyone but *you* had found it, they probably would've!" Marsha agreed. "Their luck really sucks!"

"Well, your track record makes me agree you can pursue this for awhile," Paddy said. "You have the sense to drop it if it isn't going to go anywhere. You'll definitely snare the two of them, minimum.

"Now! Sign this!"

He dropped a long letter to the commissioners in front of Nick. It suggested Sgt. Marsha Blevins was one royal pain in the ass to Capt. James and the officers at South Station, and that she'd be far better suited to a job downtown, or maybe even at the county building. She was qualified to hold a much higher position than that of Paddy's aide.

Not in those words.

Nick grinned and signed it below Jim's, Shirley's, and

Dolly's neat signatures.

"Ah! This will guarantee Marsh stays right the hell here!" Paddy said. "The commissioners seem to be rather, er, irritated with Sgt. Blevins, myself, and my officers for some reason. They won't miss this chance to get back at us!

"I must wonder why they appear to *not* wish to have such a highly qualified officer working right there with them *every day* where she can see what they're doing firsthand?"

"Well, they have to raise her pay and rank, while they can't leave her here if they do – according to the rules they passed last summer in an effort to screw each other over. I wonder how they'll handle such a dilemma?"

"It's a good thing I mentioned that part about them making the rule that we couldn't spend so much of our time on such non-essential tasks as appearing before their stupid wasteful political meetings, so they could change it, couldn't they?" Marsha said, innocently. "I think I phrased it a bit more diplomatically."

"Aha! Maybe a wee bit differently, but *not* more diplomaticly!" Paddy pointed out. "Well, back to the vastly overpaid and underworked grind!"

Nick grinned at them, winked at Marsh, and went back into the main station. Dolly was busy collecting sheets from the fax, so he didn't bother her. He had four plus hours until his regular shift began. He went home to spend time with his wife and son. He wasn't going to think about his case until he was back on duty.

Jan was planning Frog's wedding. He played with little Cole until time for his dinner, which he always ate at around five o'clock so he'd be ready for work at six. He was used to that schedule.

There was a thick stack of fax paper on his desk, meaning Dolly's search had turned up something to occupy his time, if nothing else. She had sorted it into three sections, and had added an outline for each one. That would save him time!

First was for Lyle N. Posten. He'd lived what seemed a reasonably normal life until he'd started a business with Downs. It was to be a local advertiser, but it grew into telemarketing as that became more and more popular. It operated along fairly honest lines until he married Suzanne Marie Long, then had steadily gone more and more into charity scams.

Not much. He'd made a lot of money.

Next, Suzanne Marie Long wasn't traceable until she married Posten. She was originally from Dennison, Illinois, according to the copy of the marriage certificate. She seemed a normal sort of bimbo.

That meant time to be spent. He had to know a lot about her.

Downs and Posten were parallel since high school, except Downs was always at the fringes of trouble without getting into much more than minor things. This didn't tell him much of anything. It would have to be dug out with legwork. Tomorrow.

Chapter five

The person the least was known about was Suzanne, so Nick would concentrate on her first.

She was born Suzanne Marie Long June 17, 1969, in Dennison, Illinois, according to her driver's license. Dolly didn't have anything about her childhood in the faxes. Nick used the net to ask for her records. Forty two minutes later he was informed there was no one of that name in the Dennison area birth records within three years of that date, either way.

Vedddy inderesdink!

He asked for property records for anyone named Long in that period, then for records of births among those people. Nothing quite fit. The one possibility was traced and was living in Chicago, married to someone named Fenzic.

She would have attended grammar school starting about 1974 or 1975. He checked the records of that. She was there. Child of the Marvin Longs.

There were no births to the Marvin Long family at the time she would have been born. What was going on?

Lonnie Micks, close friend of Nick, and the one whose home was to be used for Frog and Dolly's marriage, came in to find Nick tapping himself on the side of the head with a lead pencil and muttering.

"What's up?" Lonnie asked.

"How did this little girl, daughter of two people who never had any children, start school in nineteen seventy four?"

"Oh. One of those puzzle questions that're so obvious you miss the answer!" Lonnie laughed. "I know that one! Because the kid was adopted!"

"Lord, I'm stupid!"

"That's what those mind-twist puzzles are for. They're so obvious, yet you never can think of the answer.

"We're going out to Jim's Sunday. Frog and Dolly are invited. Our little crowd's growing!"

Jim Hill, fellow officer, lived on a gulf barrier island. Most of the crew and a few close friends spent most Sundays at his place.

"Are Drums and Annette coming out? I believe they're on hiatus now. I hear Annette's doing vocals with Dave on some things. Dan said you'd think it was Fleetwood Mac if you weren't where you could see them."

Drums was the drummer for the famous hard rock band, "Not So Hard Times" and a regular member of the group who met at Jim's. Annette was his wife.

"She's got a good voice for duets, but not for solos. I think they're playing a big charity concert in Orlando. Serena's working, but I'll be there."

"Isn't she getting late for working?"

"No. She has more than a month to go, and she refuses to take her maternity leave yet. She wants to use as much as she can after the kid's born. I make enough for us, but she says nursing's in her blood, and she isn't about to give it up. The hospital's got a good childcare center. She can work and be there at the same time."

They chatted a few minutes. Lonnie was on his way home and saw Nick's car at the station, so stopped in. He had to do a little bit of grocery shopping on the way home. He left when Nick got a return call from Viki at the insurance company. She had a note to call him.

"What information do you have on Suzanne Long-Posten I don't have in the stuff you already gave me? I didn't find any birth records, which would probably mean she was adopted. I can trace everyone else pretty well, but she's got big gaps in her records."

"I have all that stuff in the comp. Give me a second." There was about a two minute wait, then, "She was the child of Marvin and Gladys Long, Dennison. I see that she attended

Benjamin Franklin grammar school, Forester Junior High, as they called them then, and Blakely High. I can't find ... she didn't graduate high school, but finished all four years because ... she was on suspension for a minor morals charge of some sort, but the record of that is sealed.

"She was married to ... William D. Standing, Houston, Texas. Nineteen eighty seven to ... nineteen eighty seven? I don't know what this ... no divorce. Married Posten in eighty nine.

"Hmm! I think I want to know what happened to hubby number one! Why no divorce?"

"Houston? I can find that, I think. You said her husband was William D. Standing? S - T - A - N - D - I - N - G? Do you have what the D's for?"

"No. Married in Houston February fourteen eighty seven in a civil ceremony. It's all I have."

"I'll get back to you! I have something to work on, at least. This could get interesting yet! Later!"

She said goodbye and hung up. Nick went to Dolly's desk and asked her to find what happened to Standing, and gave her what information he had, then went back to his desk to trace a thing or two about Downs and Poston, but didn't find much of anything unexpected.

Paddy and Marsha were going to lunch. He and Dolly joined them. Nick was going to spend a couple of hours on a stakeout of Posten's place to see who came and went, after lunch, then he'd decide whether to go back home before the regular shift or to work through.

"Should I put Ellen on your shift?" Paddy asked.

"To tell the truth, I don't know. I've yet to figure where this thing might go!"

"She wants the overtime," Marsha suggested. "Put her on for tonight, then you can decide about tomorrow night tomorrow."

They decided to do that. Paddy, Marsha, and Dolly went

back to the office while Nick went to sit down the block from Posten's little Naples hideaway. Nobody came or went at Posten's place for three hours. Nick went home.

"Dolly left a pile of stuff on your desk," Marsha greeted, as Nick clocked in. "Ellen will be here at eight. We can work it in as legitimate overtime if she works less than six hours of your shift without so much paperwork. Paddy's gone. I'm just here to change my name tag."

"Your what?"

"Seeing I'm not Sgt. M. Blevins anymore, I can't keep using that one. And after I paid three bucks for the thing a measly four years ago!"

"Lieutenant?"

"*Specialist* M. Blevins! I've earned a promotion. They don't dare give me a standard type, or I have to be transferred to where I'd be working directly with them, thusly, and so they decided to create a new rank. Specialist!

"It has the full lieutenant's pay, perks and rank, but is a permanent position because I work so very efficiently with Paddy and my fellow officers. Your little petition to get my ass out of here worked like a charm. They've put me here *permanently*, and even *they* can't do one single solitary damned thing about it. I'm here as long as Paddy stays, and they can't do one single solitary damned thing about Paddy without causing a public riot. They figured getting him hooked up on a permanent basis with me, who he indicated he hates passionately, will fix his little red wagon, but *good*!

"Like shooting fish in a barrel!"

"I wish my case was as easy as those clowns, but it's mostly vastly confused. Maybe Dolly found something I can use."

He picked up the sheets and sat back to read: In 1986 William Dorset Standing appeared full-blown on the Houston money market scene. Little was known about him, except that he had a certain amount of funds and a flair for turning little sums into big ones in short time. The later investigation (!) indicated he was from the Chicago area, but nothing was ever determined as certain.

He was about 6'1" in height, 180 pounds, med/dark hair, brown eyes, wore glasses, and spoke with an educated use of English and Spanish. He was also heard to speak Japanese and German. He had invested about thirty two thousand dollars in cash, then moved into various ventures with floating funds or on borrowed guarantees.

Suzanne Marie Long met and married him. Their courtship, if there was one, was very short. After almost one year in Houston, Standing and two million dollars in secured cash disappeared. It later turned out the bonds used for security were on option, not owned by Standing. Some banks took a bath.

Suzanne Marie Long-Standing (Nick giggled at that one) filed for an annulment and went back home, met Posten, they dated for about three months, and got married.

Nick shuffled through the papers for the faxed pictures of Suzanne and Standing from their wedding photo. He was a smoothie type, sported a Van Dyke, and showed perfect teeth. He seemed dark, but that could be the picture – although Suzanne wasn't dark, and was in the same photo. There was some nagging reason that struck Nick. He studied the picture awhile.

The hands weren't as dark as the face.

Nick tried to draw Standing without the goatee, but wasn't nearly a good enough artist. He swore just as Ellen came in. She asked what it was about.

"Can you sketch?"

"No, but I can use the computer program. Paddy got Dolly that program that makes a sketch for you. I'm learning to use it."

"Good! Let's see if maybe we can take the beard and mustache off of this joker! Do you think we could?"

"That should be easy enough. Put the photo in the scanner and I'll run it onto CD, then we can experiment without worrying we'll lose it."

She showed Nick how to scan the photo and transfer it to the screen. She could box out any part of the photo and enlarge it to any size she wanted. She blocked Standing's head and made it a full screen picture.

"Now. The program will put hair on, so it'll take hair off! Let me read the manual."

She read for about ten minutes, then typed in an order and punched "Enter" – and nothing happened.

She read a little more, then took the mouse and punched the activator key, moving it back and forth around the mustache and beard. It erased the facial hair and left a dotted line where the jaw and chin line would be.

"I'll be damned! Can you change the hair to a dirty brown and change the hairline? Give it more of a widow's peak and a slightly higher forehead?"

"It's Posten?" she asked, selecting the F7 key and watching the palette appear. "Which shade?"

Nick selected the shade he wanted. She clicked the mouse on it, then moved the cursor to the hair and clicked on the mouse again. The hair was the shade Nick had chosen, complete to the proper shadows and highlights.

"Setting the hairline means you have to use the stylus, and I'm no good at that. Maybe we can select the hairstyle, I think. Yes. F four!"

She punched F4 and a batch of 30 pictures of hairlines came on the screen. Nick said it was number 22 or 23.

She pushed Alt and held it while she selected #22. The picture had that hairline in place.

"Like a photo I took today!"

"It's Posten?"

"Nope! It's Downs!"

"The guy Posten's in business with? His wife's lover? The

one who collects all those insurance claims?"

"The same!"

Concentrating on Suzanne had given him a direction of sorts, at least. He could figure ... what?

"What a ridiculous stupid mess! Is she behind it? Is he? Are they? Who knows what about whom?

"I thought this was going to turn into fun when we turned up with the picture of Downs, but all it did was to tie another knot in our ... yo. I'll drop the metaphors that never work for me, anyhow. I can usually see where something's going, but this is something that keeps going in circles."

"I'm glad it's your case!" Ellen agreed, with feeling. "It isn't just circular, it's moebus! I don't even know which circle any of them are in.

"Nickie me boy, I think you'd be smart to grab Friend Posten on the insurance fraud and suspicion of murder and Downs on the same charges. You can hope they'll do something that ties her tail in a knot, but you can't win 'em all!

"I know. The fact she used to be married to Downs means you can grab them all, but they can then use each other to put the murder on somebody else. A jury would say you'd proved fraud. They won't really get away with it, so they'd just as soon drop the murder part.

"I think you've found the one that'll get away!"

"And I think I can manage to put a stop to this stupid crap if I keep digging. It will depend on one other little base factor. If it's not there, I'm in trouble."

"Which is?"

"*One* of them doesn't know what's going on with the other two!" Nick smirked.

"Which one?" she asked, after thinking for a moment.

"That's the rub. That's what I have to find out. Maybe I can scare that one into admitting something.

"This is the part of detective work they always leave out of the books and news reports. It's legwork time!"

She grinned and went to her desk to study the users' manual on the computer ID sketch program, then called to Nick to ask if she should get in touch with Houston to see if they held a warrant for Downs/Standing. Nick thought it over. He agreed that might turn up something else, but they'd have to agree to wait to act.

Nick took out his chart, started to fill in some boxes, then stopped. Even his trusty old box chart wasn't going to help with this one. It was making it even more confusing.

Or was it?

He filled in the boxes, adding a sheet above to handle the earlier years.

Downs and Posten had gone to high school together, then had gone their separate ways for a few years, keeping in touch, and had gone into business together.

Before or after Houston? He went through the files. Before.

So! Did Posten know about Houston? That his wife was once the wife of his business partner? Did Downs start planning this years ago?

Downs had two million dollars when he left Texas. Why would he get into something like this for a few more lousy millions? Why wasn't two million enough for him? He'd used the money to set himself up in business, but the business was paying, judging by its expansions and by the way he lived.

Crooked businesses. He could have gone legitimate and made as much or more, so why ... *anything?*

There was something very big he didn't know. There had to be. He needed a break, and he needed it soon. Ellen was far too right about this one getting away from him.

Nick sighed deeply and punched a telephone number from memory. It reached Pancho DeGulio, the friend who gave him the Martinique vacation place. The man who knew everything there was to know about the major crime bosses in the US.

"Nickie!" Pancho greeted. "How good to hear from you!"

"I was speaking with Jan. She invited me to the wedding of Frog and Dolly. I will come."

"Thanks, Pancho, it wouldn't be much of a wedding without you. I'll insist they take their honeymoon at the place on Martinique.

"I'm afraid I'm calling now to ask for some information."

"Jan said you have a case that's got you acting like you did with that hospital thing. I know nothing about those people, I'm afraid."

"You know about the case? Who it involves?"

"No. Which is why I know nothing about them. Had it concerned any of the people in the higher circles, I would automatically be informed. I have received no inquiries or information whatever.

"Perhaps Arturo would know something. They are from an area where he does a great deal of business."

They chatted a few minutes, then Nick hung up and sat back.

"Were you just talking to one of those drug lords or crime lords? Paddy goes nuts when you do that!"

"Pancho DeGulio. He's not a crime or drug lord, just a very smart friend. This one is a crime boss. The biggest!"

He picked up the phone again and punched a second number from memory. Ellen looked interested, but said nothing.

"Arturo? Nick. How're things in the big city?"

"Nick! Cold, wet, dirty, and boring," Arturo Doniletti said, heartily. "Good to hear from you! Business or social?

"Greco's here! It's Nick, the cop, Greco! I'll put it on the speaker if I can figure how to work the damned thing. Ahh!"

"It's mostly business, but I wanted to say hello. I have a case that I can't figure the angles on. The people are from near the Chicago area. Greco might be in a much better position to know anything.

"Did you ever hear of a Lyle Posten?"

"Posten? What's he into?" Arturo asked.

"Scams. Telemarketing stuff, mostly. Insurance fraud, but that might be a new venture."

"Not me. Greco?"

"Never heard of 'im."

"William Standing or Wayne Downs? Same?"

"No."

"Suzanne Long?"

"Looker? Flashy? Sort of dumb actin'?" Greco asked.

"Yeah."

"Heard of her. She took Louie Roberts for one hell of a load a couple of years ago. He wanted to get her cut up or somethin' for revenge. Got over it. She ran off to Texas with some high school lover. Hit Louie for thirty five or forty grand. It wasn't the money so much as his pride.

"If she's in the phone charity scams, she learned that from Louie. He thought he was in love or some such crap and let her get her hands on some things. She left with some crap he didn't dare to chase her if she had, if you get the drift. That's why he dropped it. She gets grief, he gets grief. Mexican standoff, but he'd hit her in a minute if he could get away with it.

"Ask me, he'd take one look and start kissin' her ass again. Louie don't have any brains when that type wiggles 'em in his face."

"Penny-ante!" Arturo agreed. "Louie's one of the bunch that *don't* come to social functions where I'm attending.

"I'm beginning to get class, Nick. That kind of woman brings out the low, women like Donna bring out the high. Tell Jan I'm another one she can start planning a wedding for! You think Lonnie would let me get married at his place like Pancho did? Tell Jan I promise there won't be no goons there!"

Jan had once told Arturo he could stay, but she wanted his goons out of her house. He thought that took a lot of guts and had liked her ever since.

"I'll ask, just to see what he says, but you have to ask him yourself."

"Yeah. I will! Lonnie'n me get along good," Arturo replied, with a laugh. "I'll worry about bringing Donna to his place the way women act around him."

"He's married now. He doesn't sleep around anymore," It was a joke how women constantly chased Lonnie, who used to accommodate them. He became a one woman man the minute he married Serena.

"Yeah – and he means it! Damnedest thing I ever saw! They say it's all right if Lonnie tells them to take a hike, because he's married and doesn't screw around anymore!"

They talked a minute longer, then said their goodbyes. Nick lounged back.

"Arturo Doniletti, the most powerful crime lord in the whole country and several others?"

"*And* Greco Miklokaras, second most powerful! It seems wifey dear has a bit of a history. Nice girl!"

"But did you learn anything?"

"No. Yes. I learned it started a little earlier than I first thought, but it still doesn't fit. Something's missing from the equation. I think I'll go stake out Suzanne. Either she'll go to see Posten or Downs will come to see her. I want to check on that annulment, just to be sure."

He called Houston records on the internet. Suzanne didn't get an annulment anywhere in Texas. She had filed one, but never came in to have the court action certified. She was, as a direct result, still married to Standing/Downs. Legally.

"Darker and a lot muddier!" Nick exclaimed, grinned, saluted, and headed for the Pointe.

Three hours of watching and nothing at all happened.

Suzanne didn't leave and no one came. Her car sat right in front of the door the whole time. Nick was about ready to give it up when Downs' car pulled in and stopped by the door. Suzanne got out and went into the house and Downs drove off. Nick started to swear, then giggled. Watching the place where the subject wasn't was almost as boring as watching the place where the subject was, it seemed.

Nick went home to his wife and kid.

Chapter six

"Hey, Nick?" Ellen suddenly said. She'd just answered a call on the line and had the phone mouthpiece covered.

"Yo?"

"Didn't one of your suspects live on Hutton Place just off of Juanita?"

"Four thirty two," Nick answered, perking up. "Why?"

She pointed to the phone and stuck up three fingers. Nick punched 3 and carefully picked up the receiver.

"Mr. Small, slow down!" Ellen ordered. "You say someone tried to drown you? Stop. Think very carefully, then tell me exactly what happened. Talk slowly."

"I was out by the pool. I dozed off, and the next thing I knew I was in the water. I've been hit over the head! They just dumped me in the pool and I almost drowned!"

"How did they get in? Isn't there an enclosure? Was it locked?" Ellen asked. "Is there anything missing that would indicate burglary was involved?"

"I came to when I went under. I came up. They ran out. There doesn't seem to be anything missing. There isn't anything here to steal!

"I'm calming down now. I can think a little clearer.

"Let's see. I went to sleep beside the pool, about seven or so, and it's now ... ten twenty. I woke up in the water, under it, as a matter of fact. I was being *held* under! I remember that I flailed a bit. And hitting someone's hand against the side of the pool, then they let me go and I came up. They were just running out through the screen door into the side yard."

"Mr. Small, if there was no burglary, someone must have gone there deliberately to kill you," Ellen said. "Who knew you'd be there? Who has reason to want you dead?"

"But *nobody* knows where I am, and no one has any reason

to try to *kill* me!"

"Apparently, they do! To both! Mr. Small, I want you to be certain you're fully alert and aware and that you can defend yourself if the attacker returns before I arrive. Do you have a weapon in the house?"

"No, other than kitchen knives and so forth. I'm pretty big. I can handle myself."

"Are you bulletproof, Mr. Small? I want you to lock that house up tight and find a place where you are not visible from anywhere outside. Find something you can use as a club and listen for sounds of intrusion. If you hear anything odd you are to station yourself immediately outside of the door or entrance to that room and to the side. If *anyone* comes through that door, hit fast, and wonder who and why later!

"I will announce my name – loudly – when I arrive. I am Lt. Ellen Vickers. Do *not* open the door for *anyone* else!

"What is my name?"

"Lt. Ellen Vickers."

"I'll be there within ten minutes. Secure that house!"

"Yes ma'am!"

She hung up and said "C'mon!" to Nick.

"This is the break I need! They have to get rid of him, for some reason. He'll be ready to give them to me on a platter!" Nick exulted, as they headed for a cruiser. "Maybe I can make some sense out of it with his help."

They screamed into the drive at 432 with lights and sirens blaring. Ellen ran to the door and rang the bell, calling out loudly, "Lt. Ellen Vickers, Mr. Small!"

No one answered. Nick ran around the side of the house and in through the pool enclosure's screen door. The door to the house was open, and he yelled, "Mr. Small! Police! Lt. Nick Storie and Lt. Ellen Vickers! Are you all right?"

No answer. Nick drew his sidearm as he moved quickly inside, he checked each room to the side as he went quickly to the front door to open it for Ellen.

"He's gone?" Ellen asked.

Nick nodded, and went through the kitchen to the garage to find no car inside. Suzanne had driven up, used the automatic opener on the door, and driven in. He didn't have a car.

He stopped to think, then reached up to place his hand on the door motor. It was cold.

"It seems he thought it over. If we come here, we ask questions he doesn't want to answer – such as; how come he's the recently deceased Lyle Posten?

"He didn't have a car. He left on foot. He can't be far. Not in ten minutes.

"He doesn't dare come back here again. If we don't return, a business partner or wife might. Either way is disastrous, so far as Lyle Posten is concerned.

"We don't know enough about him, El. We can't hope to figure what he'll do."

"So we secure the house and file a report. Next time you grab them when you have the chance. Paddy will get all over you for that."

"No. He knows I didn't have much choice there. This still means it's fallen apart. I think he'll not let Downs or Suzanne get a hint of where he goes – and he can strap at least one of them in the chair. They'll be awfully nervous.

"Maybe it's not as bad as it looked, at first. Let's print this place until we have a good set of Posten's and his wife's. If we also find Downs' prints in this house, all hell's gonna break loose!"

Ellen grinned and went to the cruiser for the kit. This would be the perfect excuse to prove Posten was alive for the insurance companies, too.

There were several sets of prints inside the house. The best were on dishes and glasses and doorknobs. The knob to the screen enclosure had no prints at all. Those had been wiped, or the intruder wore gloves.

They had Posten's prints – that Dr. Akins had *not* tried to match to the body of Mathews. They had Downs' prints from his stint in Texas as Standing, but they didn't have Suzanne's.

Yes, they did! She'd been arrested, according to several of their sources. Hers would be easy to obtain without asking her to allow printing.

They finished at the house, locked it up tight, and went back to the forensics lab with the prints. Comparisons quickly showed that Posten had definitely been there. Nick had Suzanne's prints faxed in, but Downs' weren't found in the house.

Nick sat back to think a bit, then grinned to himself and informed Ellen he was going to call on Suzanne with the news her dear departed husband – the second – was alive.

"You're not going to face her with the fact we also have her prints there? What's the deal?"

"I'll tell her we found other prints in the house and are having them processed. Let's see where she runs this time!"

"You'll tell her we know she was married to Wayne Downs and never got a divorce?"

"No way! Not about the lack on an annulment from *Standing*! I'll leave her knowing that we plan to check into that part tomorrow, when the record departments are open."

"Which leaves her until they open to get the hell out or to make up a story!" She matched Nick's grin. "This one's getting more toward being fun again, isn't it?"

"Well, it's getting to where we can do a little bit of the manipulating, for a change. Fun, this one ain't! Not by any criterion!"

Nick went to his car and drove to the Pointe. Suzanne's car was in the drive. So was Down's. Nick grinned to himself as he sauntered to the door to ring the bell. Downs came to the door to tell him it was a bit late. Suzanne wouldn't be receiving guests tonight.

"Oh, this isn't social. I've come to tell her we found her husband. He made a call to us to report someone tried to kill him, a bit earlier. Don't count on getting any insurance payoffs. You'll have to return the ones already collected."

He looked startled and a bit scared. He stepped aside and said for Nick to come on in. Suzanne was standing in a door to the side with a hand held to her throat – which reminded Nick. He looked at their hands, but saw no scraping or bruising on any of them.

"My husband? He's called you? Are you sure? It was definitely him and not a trick?"

"Yes. Your second husband, Lyle Norton Posten, is alive and well – alive at least – or was only a couple of hours ago. He called us to say he'd been attacked at the house where he was staying on Hutton Place. He was able to thwart the attempt then, but was afraid there might be a repeat. We went directly there, but he was gone."

"Then how in the unholy hell do you know it was Posten?" Downs demanded sarcastically. "Some joker calls and claims to be Posten and you immediately assume he's for real? Are YOU for real?"

"Oh, no!" Nick laughed. "He said his name was Small, when he called us. We went out there to rescue someone named Small and found out later it was Posten. Another officer and I went to the house. He was gone. We did the routine printing. There was no sign of struggle or violence, but we *had* been called, and an attempted murder complaint *was* entered, so we followed normal procedures. We found several good sets of prints inside the house. His were already put in the lab computer where we'd been comparing them with those of the body, Mathews, that was found in Posten's car.

"Mathews, who worked for you, Mr. Downs. We've now positively identified him as being the DB in Poston's car. That will be great fun for you to explain, I'll bet!

"Anyhow, those prints were already online, locally, and made a very fast match. Lyle Norton Posten was Small, or vice versa. We'll turn that information over to the insurers who issued the policies on him in the morning. We'll also run those other prints from that house through the IID net and to Washington. We'll know who they belong to fairly soon.

"We've got you, Downs. The insurance fraud scam is as solid as anything ever could be, but I'm going to tag you for murder one for Mathews. I'll turn the insurance business over to fraud in the morning, when I give it to the insurers.

"If there's one print from you in that house, it ties you as accessory before the fact – which is the same thing. You'd better run! Murder one isn't some game where you outsmart the good guys. It's permanent.

"Trouble there! We'll be watching every move you two make! We'll find who else is in this mess from those prints, no doubt.

"Mrs. Posten, there seems to be a serious question about the legality of your marriage to Posten. When the court records are available in the morning, we'll know if you ever got around to finalizing the annulment. If not, you'd be smart to gather everything you can prove is solely your property around here and be prepared to be removed from Posten's property.

"You may deduce I don't think you ever bothered with such a trivial detail. We're going to get everything that's known about your life with Standing and about Standing himself. It seems he was suddenly there, then suddenly gone. That usually means it was just a setup to steal money, in these cases.

"We have computers now. We'll find out exactly who Standing really is, and exactly where he is."

"If he isn't Bill Standing, or wasn't, I'd sure like to know it! I don't know how you could find him after this long!"

Something suddenly occurred to Nick. It might throw a bit

more of a scare into both of them. It was certainly worth a try. It might even be true.

"Oh, because of something else we have now. DNA testing. The world's catching up to the best of the scams faster than you can come up with new ones."

"Oh, and how would you obtain any DNA from this Standing to compare?" Downs sneered. "You don't seem too intent on all those details you accuse Suzanne of over-looking, do you?"

"He got married. In Texas. They took a blood sample for the tests. They still have it. I'd better get back to the station. I think you're going down for the big one, Downs. I think just maybe Mrs. Posten isn't standing there with particularly clean hands, herself. Maybe you'll have company.

"Have a nice evening! When we collect all our facts tomorrow it may make it your last chance in this lifetime!"

Downs and Suzanne looked like two people who had just been hit over the head with something very nasty. Nick went down the road to park, looking back at the house. He called for a surveillance car to meet him there. Nothing happened for almost an hour, then the boat left the dock behind the house and headed for the gulf. Nick and Sgt. Vic Demarco hurried to the house, but there was no one there.

Nick called Marine Patrol, but there wouldn't be an officer close this time of night.

"Why am I always one tiny step behind and confused with this one?" Nick demanded of no one. He sighed heavily and told Vic to keep an eye on the house. He went to the station. There was no word from anyone when he went home at the end of his shift.

"We're still looking for the boat," Jim said. "There doesn't seem to be any way they could hide something that big, but you never know.

"One thing's sure! If they've headed out to the islands or

Mexico or something, you'll play hell finding them, then even more hell getting them extradited.

"Lonnie's bringing you guys out day after tomorrow. I don't think you should let this case ruin your Sunday. Finish it today and tomorrow.

"Did you see that crab act on the TV?"

"Crab act? On TV?" Nick asked.

"Those two half-assed commissioners. They're trying – hard – to find a way to rescind their last restructuring of the advancement system of county employees. It seems they'd made a rule, debated it, and passed it unanimously, and now learn it ties their hands to where they can't give advances in salaries or grade without a full meeting in those few special occasions that sometimes present themselves in the everyday business of running the governing of...."

"Okay! I didn't see it. What's it really about?"

"Seems Halliday wants to put her brother on the new appropriations review and recommendations board, but has to get the agreement of the other four commissioners. Fat chance! There's no way Johnson's going to let her pull that! Not since Halliday caused the big stink that got Johnson's wife's little sister dumped from the zoning compliance board!

"See, they passed the bill in such a way that they have to all agree before it can be changed while every decision concerning employment in any commission controlled positions must be unanimous, brethren!

"That was to thwart Nancy Ann Starkle (Owner of a local news tabloid that was a sharp thorn in the side of the commissioners et al) when she wants to put pressure on one or two of them she has the goods on. They can claim they *can't* do what she demands because the *others* refuse.

"You see, they wanted to make absolutely sure a certain Sgt. M. Blevins didn't get access to their private doings, which is right where the promotion she was due would put her. They made up a very quick bill and passed it. That law created a specialty category of the aides of police station captains. Each one put in a bit of goody for himself or herself, and they got carried away. The bill had more riders than a dude ranch. What's good for the gander can sometimes cook somebody elses' goose, it seems."

"You ask me it can cook the gander's goose!" Marsha, who had come from Paddy's office, suggested. "I hear your prime suspects have flown the coop, Nick. Was that part of the plan?"

"Hell, no!"

"You will *never* be a successful politician!" Marsha chided. "The answer was, `Of course!' Later it could be somebody elses' fault it didn't go where you thought it would. *They* screwed up your months of careful diligent thought and labor!

"What now?"

"I'll put this information together and tie everything up as tight as I can. I can get the warrants ready to be served when we find them."

"What if they don't come back?" Jim asked.

"They'll come back. There's one very good reason I know that!"

"What?" Marsha asked.

"Money. The whole thing was about money. They'll be back as sure as we're sitting here. They might have had a few thousand, even as much as a million, at the house, but I rather sincerely doubt it. There's a lot of money somewhere they'll be back for."

"I don't have anything right now," Jim said. "Want to try to find it? We could get to it first and be waiting when they get back. It'll be in cash, I suppose?"

"Yeah. It'll be in cash or held under an alias, I imagine. Downs likes aliases. We can get Dolly to start looking through whatever comp records she can legally find in local bank records or stock transactions. There might be a bunch of valuable bearer bonds held somewhere. Downs was tied up with that market in Texas when he was Standing. She can give us copies of his picture. We might even find he has some safe deposit boxes."

"Standing where?" Jim asked. "We can get the warrants for all his business properties through the fraud thing."

"He used the name Standing in Texas. I think he was going to....!"

"Uh-oh!" Marsha said. "You just solved something! I'd know that sudden stop anywhere!"

"I just figured a thing or two. I didn't quite understand several people's reactions to things, now I think I do! I'm not working confused anymore. He is not getting away with it! I promise you that! He is *not* getting away with it! Party time is *over*!

"Okay, let's find the money, Jim. I think we have a case of a double-cross to end all double-crosses! I really do! The mouse just turned into the cat, but the original cat doesn't know it yet!"

"You don't make sense!" Jim said. He called Dolly to come in and they got their pictures, then set out to find how much money was secreted around, and where it was hidden.

Nick handed Dolly a sheet. She read it over, said, "I'll be damned!" and moved to her terminal. Nick picked up several more pictures from his desk and headed for his car. Jim would take the southern part of the county and Nick the northern. Dolly would cover the whole country with her computer links.

Nick headed for the bank farthest north and east, the First Collier Union, and spoke with the woman in charge of the safety deposit boxes and the manager. He handed them a copy of a search warrant Marsha had from Judge Collins. None of them had anything there. Security Trust, the same. Loyalty Savings and Loan had an account in the name of

LSP Promotions, Inc. which had a hundred forty five thousand in it. There was a safety deposit box under the name of Posten that they opened, after calling a recorder from the court. It was empty.

Twelve banks and four deposit box openings later Nick went back to the station. Jim was coming off shift and gave him the records from the nine banks he'd covered before he got a call and had to break from Nick's case for three plus hours, a little past noon. Jim had found three empty boxes in the name of Posten and two with jewelry, money, bonds, CDs and deeds in the names of Suzanne Posten and Wayne Downs.

"So. He had a bunch of cash he took out before the body ever turned up in his Porsche," Jim said. "Does that change anything, really?"

"When you consider a thing or two, yes. Did you wonder why there was no money in the Small house on Hutton? We're talking several million – at least! Where is it?"

"I see!" Marsha suddenly said. "*He* set the whole scheme up all by himself and roped his wife and Downs into it. Suzanne and Downs were running a scam with fraud and charity rip-offs, but *Posten* brought murder into it.

"Then why did Suzanne know where he was?"

"She *is* an airheaded bimbo!" Jim said. "*She* had to lead us to *him*. Why?"

"Why, how else would we know he was alive and that she and Downs were murderers? If we didn't find a way to prove he's still alive he'd never be rid of them.

"He had a box in the name of Small in Unity Trust, only six blocks from the place on Hutton. There's going to be another DB – almost certainly Posten – and it will be obvious murder. I think our making Suzanne and Downs run put a little crink in his plans. If they're to kill him, they have to be HERE!"

Dolly came over to drop a fax sheet on his desk.

"You figured that one! Key West. It seems a Mr. Parker bought a small cottage on Arrowhead Key."

"Posten?" Marsha asked.

"Yes. Small made three separate trips to Key West in the past four months – before there was any Mr. Small! Nick had me trace, using a fax of his picture. I found airline reservations under the name of Small, then sent faxes of his picture to the destinations. Nick said to check realtors. He'd want to lay low for awhile, then would probably set himself up in business again. He's owned the Hutton place for over a year. I have the sheriff down there waiting to greet him!"

Paddy had come in to listen. "What about those two on that boat? Shall I have fraud file on them?"

"I did that this morning," Marsha said.

"Damnit to hell! Maybe I should have thought over not letting the commissioners get you out of here!" Paddy replied,with a huge smile. "Joan and Hank are meeting us at Italia Bellissima in about twenty minutes. Move it!"

"They are?" Marsha said.

"If you're running the office now, I get to run the social calendar. I have to do SOMETHING around here!"

She gave him the finger salute. Jim grinned and headed home, Dolly laughed and went out. Marsha and Paddy left, and Nick was alone in the office.

He got out his box chart.

Chapter seven

"Where will you find Posten?" Nick asked himself. "He's been a step or two ahead, so far!"

He sighed heavily and revised his chart to fit what he now suspected. He didn't much like these cases that were so stupidly complicated by clever people. They wasted far too much time. Clever people always seemed to outsmart themselves before it was over.

Posten did that. He shouldn't have added that extra detail about hitting the attacker's hand against the side of the pool. It meant either Suzanne would have to be the attacker or she would have had to have paid someone else to do it. When there were no prints from Downs in the house, that was all that was left. Suzanne couldn't have hired a hit man to do it because a professional wouldn't have done anything so sloppily it would leave him alive. Posten would be dead.

There were no marks anywhere on her hands or lower arms, ergo, the pale-skinned Suzanne hadn't had her hands hit onto the side of any concrete pool, ergo, there was no attack.

Nick thought about the phony crime scene by the pool, pictured what he'd seen, and nodded to himself. There was one big splash of wetness beside an overturned plastic and aluminum chaise lounge where someone might have been dumped in, and a trail from the steps to the side where someone had left the pool and gone into the house. Had he been dumped into the pool at the splash, his attacker would have had to position himself in that puddle to hold him under, and would have left a decided trail of footprints to the enclosure door when he ran out.

There was no trail. There was no attacker. Therefore, Posten had the money packed and ready, or he had it out and in another hiding place long before he tried this latest stunt.

He would go to the money. He also must come up with another body, this one to undeniably be his. There wouldn't be anymore insurance, but he'd want to make sure no one would be looking for him.

How would he work it, and could Nick hope to find him?

The place in the Keys was by far his best hope. The sheriff in the area would grab him as soon as he appeared. That left Suzanne and Downs. Suzanne had been used all along. She was enough of an airhead for him to be able to make up any number of stories that make himself seem to be innocent. She probably *had* been in Ft. Myers shopping when Hawk Mathews was killed. Downs had to be in it deep. He supplied Mathews.

But for what?

Nick thought awhile, then used the IID net to have a picture of Mathews faxed to him. Mathews looked very much like Posten, in general size and shape. The basic features were pretty much like Posten's, but the hair was different and the shape of the ears and lips. The data with the picture showed that Mathews had done some work in commercials and as a singer with a pop band, but wasn't successful with the music part, because his voice was "pleasantly modulated and able enough" but was "not suitable" to the popular styles, being more of the type appreciated "before 1960" or for jazz.

His work in commercials led to minor parts in various local theater productions, but he much preferred work in the fields of horticultural and botanical research, where his work record was "above average" in acceptance.

Downs wasn't the killer type. Mathews was being set up for some other reason altogether, but what? A scam?

The acting would help there, but what was the incentive for Mathews to get off the sauce if such was to be? What kind of scam?

A 9-1-1 call came in about a domestic argument that became a fatal confrontation between a wife and her husband

and his brother. The husband was pronounced dead of multiple stab wounds. Nick went to the scene. The wife was hysterical, crying that her husband had been drunk and had attacked her, his brother had tried to separate them, and the drunk husband had pulled a knife, which the brother managed to wrestle away from him, then had to defend himself, after the husband had turned his extremely violent drunken attention on his brother.

The husband hadn't been drunk and the wife was covered with blood, while the brother had almost none on him. Tiny rolled his eyes and shook his head when he heard the woman raving on.

"I'll make my report like this," Nick suggested, when she ran down. "Your husband was coming in the door to the bedroom, right there where he's laying, and found you and his brother here. He was furious, and started yelling, which several of the neighbors will have heard. You started sticking him with that letter opener or whatever it is. You then had a body on your hands, so you made up the story and called the cops, who saw right through it.

"Anything else?"

She stared at him about three seconds, then fainted.

Nick looked at the brother. "You gonna take the heat for her so she can find some other sucker while you spend the next ten to fifteen in the pen?"

"He was supposed to be bowling tonight, but he was hiding in the house somewhere, and came in," he replied. "It was about what you said. Flo and I weren't doing anything."

"But you were going to."

"Yeah."

"You're still accessory."

"I didn't know she'd do anything like that! Honest to God! I thought I might have to kick his ass or something, but, I swear, I never thought she'd do anything like that! I mean, he's my *brother*, for Christ's sake!"

"I suppose you'll get away with probation or something such, but I really don't see you pulling that 'He's my *brother*!' act and getting any sympathy. He was also your brother when you were sleeping with his wife."

She groaned and sat up. "You are under arrest on a charge of willful murder," Nick said. "You have the right to an...."

Nick sat at his desk to read through some of the stuff Dolly had left there. Not much he didn't know or deduce. Mathews had been in some trouble in New Orleans before his alcoholism became so extreme, and had spent some time, a day or two at a clip, in the local lockup. He made bail on his last minor charge, then disappeared, turning up in Collier County, Florida.

That was three years ago. He'd done his first work for LSP almost immediately. Nick thought that was a bit too much of a coincidence. He called Pete's Palace and asked to speak to Cage. Surprisingly, he was there.

"Cage? Nick, the cop. You sober enough to tell me something?"

"Yeah, Nick. How's tricks? Got Boats' killer yet?"

"By the balls, but he doesn't know it. I need to know if Boats ever said anything about how he got his job down here.

"See, he was acting in some shows in NOLA, and was in the pen. Somebody made bail for him and he ended up here next day. He went right to work for LSP. It's a detail, but it can plug up a way out for the killer. We have to cut off all technicalities or doubts."

"The guy at Lisp made his bail. I knew him in N'Orlins, then ran into him down here. He said he had an actin' job of some sort. Later he said it was mainly a phone scam, but it was goin' to turn into something really big. Soon.

"He didn't say too much. He sorta hinted it was a big actin' job that was big pay. I told 'im he was here two years, so why didn't it already pay 'n he said it was a thing he had to do a lot of practicin' for. He said it was an improvisational act."

They talked awhile longer, then Nick hung up to sit back to consider.

The rest of his shift was quieter. He went home to Jan and Cole and had a reasonably good night's sleep, then was reading the paper while drinking his second cup of coffee. The TV was on low to entertain Cole, while Jan put things together for the trip to Jim's the following day. Nick planned to mow the lawn and clean up around the house.

"... burned almost to the waterline. The Marine Patrol and Coast Guard vessels were on the scene quickly, but an explosion made it all but certain that there would be no survivors. The mayday call came in at two fourteen this morning, and was answered immediately. Some details are being withheld until the investigation is completed, but this reporter has learned that the luxury yacht was registered to a local businessman's wife. The business partner was also aboard. There is some confusion as to who made the mayday call when the boat caught fire, as the call was purportedly from the dead man, who's wife owned the boat.

"Well, Paul! That's one for the psychic investigators!"

Nick stared at the screen, then grabbed the phone. So *that's* how he planned to do it!

Well, surprise! Surprise!, Mr. Posten!

"This is Det. Lt. Nick Storie, Naples South Station, Violent Crimes, Homicide. I have to speak with someone who is familiar with the burned boat on the TV."

The operator soon connected him with their Information Officer, Al Tibbs, who said he wasn't about to give information over the phone to anyone.

"I'm investigating the murder of D. J. Mathews, whose body was first identified as being that of Lyle Posten, who we have since proven is still alive and well. The death was an insurance fraud scheme. The fact remains that Mathews was murdered to supply the body that was then identified as Lyle Posten. If that mayday call was from Posten and his wife, Suzanne, and his business partner, Wayne Downs, were on the boat, this is another case of murder. I have to act fast on information we have about the possible whereabouts of Lyle Posten, if that's the boat that burned out there."

"I see. Under the circumstances I'm not revealing anything, merely confirming what you're saying is the case. It was the Posten boat. We have recovered the body of a Wayne Owen Downs, identified positively, and no other."

"Thanks. I'll see if I can catch Lyle N. Posten when he shows up as someone else."

"There is one other small detail you'll want to take into consideration, I'm sure. Downs was shot through the back of the head."

That wasn't expected! Nick thanked Tibbs and hung up, as Jan came to say, "You look like there's something very nasty in that coffee!"

"Not in the coffee. I think I probably won't make it out to Jim's tomorrow. Can you call Serena and have them pick you and Cole up? I may be here in the morning, I may not. I may make it back early, or it may take a day or two.

"Hon, this is one hell of a damned mess! What are they up to *now*?!

"I'll pack clothes for a couple of days, and I have to call Marsha. Paddy will go through the roof! Damn!"

He grabbed the phone again and punched the autodial for the station, then swore again and hung up. Paddy or Marsha wouldn't be there. It was Saturday.

He called Paddy at home and explained what he'd heard and what he'd done. Paddy said Shirley and Ellen were on, and Shirley could arrange a quick flight. He'd call her and see that there was a rental car waiting for him – but why New Orleans?

"That's where it started, I think. Paddy, this isn't even vaguely what we thought it was. I don't know WHAT it is! Can you have Key West just keep Posten under the best tight surveillance they can arrange? They mustn't scare him off, but they definitely mustn't let him give them the slip.

"Downs is dead, and probably Suzanne. I have to show how he got away after killing them, calling the coast guard, and firing the boat. The object is to make us believe they're ALL dead so we don't keep looking for anyone. This is an odd case, Paddy."

"Uh-huh! You keep finding all that weird stuff that doesn't have anything to do with anything. You do get the cases like that. More than anyone else, you get 'em!"

"The trouble here is that *part* of everything is part of the case and part isn't. The trouble is I keep focusing on the wrong parts. Until now.

"He'll figure, if we've found the Key West hideaway, I'll go straight there – so now I confuse *him* for a change!"

"But why New Orleans?"

"Because that's where someone met or saw or heard of someone else and started scheming. To this point, I never could figure who was what to whom or why. It's my turn!"

"Take care, Nick! I don't have time to train another officer who can see every angle my other officers would miss.

"I mean that Nick! I have a very negative feeling about this case!"

"*That's* one promise I won't forget!"

Jan packed his things and Nick headed for the airport. Next stop, New Orleans!

It was miserable in NOLa. An oily drizzle fell from a sky that was so close it looked like you could climb to the roof of the buildings and reach up into the clouds. It was much too warm for the darkness and wetness of the day.

Mathews had worked for Bordeaux Artes, which wasn't

hard to find. The manager had been the same for 9 years, and had a good memory, but she couldn't remember much of anything about some alcoholic bit actor of 3 years ago, though the picture did look slightly familiar.

"You have any idea which play? I could give you the agent who booked."

Nick had checked with the local police station and knew the date of Mathews' arrest. He was playing there at the time.

"Hmm. I recall it was a musical. Maybe it was 'Bon Mot' or one of those. Charles LeGrand (SHAR-lez luh GRAHN) books all those musicals. He'd have records." She gave him the agency's address. He headed for the place, not expecting him to be there.

"I didn't really believe you'd be in," Nick greeted, as he introduced himself.

"Why not?" LeGrand asked.

"It *is* Saturday!"

"Theater's mostly a weekend job. I'm off Tuesdays and Thursdays – when I can take any time at all. I also book bands and comics. I work weekend nights, as well. What can I do for you?"

Nick explained about the Mathews murder case and showed him the pictures. He said that he remembered Mathews. Quite well. He had a voice that would allow him to be booked with a band like the old Guy Lombardo type in a minute flat! He could have been a major "find", but didn't want it. The acting was only until he could get his act together with his regular job.

"There was a man by the name of Downs – or Standing – who may have contacted him here. He posted his bail when he left."

"I thought Susan's boyfriend put up his bail," LeGrand said, thinking. "Dwayne D. Wayne. Some sort of local advertising agent she was working for. Mathews did some work in ads. This joker owned a little ad company in Atlanta or somewhere. Paid for all that surgery on Mathews."

"Surgery?" Nick perked up at that.

"Two front teeth were like a rabbit's. Had small changes in his nose and eyes. Supposed to have had his ears flattened down or something, but that was easy to fix with makeup – and the hair. Except for the teeth, he looked much better before all that work, you ask me."

"Susan?"

"Susan Largo, a typical local slightly pretty girl who was planning to be the next Marilyn Monroe or something. We get 'em by the hundreds in this business."

Nick showed him the pictures of Downs and Suzanne.

"Mmm. Put a beard on him and change the hair, you got 'em! She could have probably made it in ads. Like Madonna, you know? Cheap as hell, but sexy!"

Nick thanked him, and soon left. He'd had all his basic questions answered – and then some! – but was more confused than ever about who was where on the chart. Suzanne's past was slowly being filled in. She was probably pretty much as LeGrand described her, a local girl who was going to take the world by storm. She got into advertising as a model, met Downs, worked the Texas scam with him, and escaped to New Orleans to lay low until the fraud cops stopped watching for him to contact her. She'd be so normal you could puke. She got a bit part in a play to tide her over until her husband came for her. She met a bit actor/drunk with that play with a truly uncanny resemblance to Downs' partner in the ad business. Downs had seized the chance to have ... *what*, damnit!? That Mathews was to become Posten all along was more than obvious, but in what capacity? *Why* was he being groomed to be Posten?

He had everything he needed from New Orleans. He picked up his ticket to Naples and exchanged it to one for Key West. He knew that, regardless of what any of this meant, he could take the sheriff at Key West and arrest Posten for several murders. He couldn't get away from those charges now, no matter what. Points about Suzanne's and Downs' motives and/or involvements were moot, at best.

Key West wasn't spectacular at night. Nick left the airport in a rented car, checked into a motel, ate a good meal, and got a good night's sleep. The deputy sheriff charged with watching for Posten to go to his little hideaway said he hadn't shown. Nick went with him to the place, about twenty miles north of Key West. They used Nick's rental car so as not to be too visible. The island wasn't very large and it was easy to find a spot where they couldn't be seen from the house to watch. Nick had learned about everyone and everything in the nearby area from John Enders, the deputy.

No one had shown at 1 o'clock. They drove to Key West for lunch. Enders then said Nick had full state authority to arrest Posten/Small so he'd get back to his regular duty, if that was alright. Nick agreed, saying he'd yell if there was any hint of trouble. He drove back to watch the place, deciding to give it the rest of the day and the next, then he'd have to figure some other angle.

He was personally sure Posten would show.

No one appeared by dark, so he went back to his motel.

The following morning he was at his spot early. Enders came at noon, bringing him a bucket of chicken. He'd bought two older SF books at the motel and was reading them while watching the place. Enders stayed a couple of hours, then headed back to Key West. Nick stayed until dark.

Well, go back home or try staking one more day? He was still certain Posten would come. One more day.

Enders came by the motel and promised he'd be with him the following afternoon. Nick asked him why he'd decided Posten would be arriving then.

"Simple! He was near Sarasota when he burned the boat. There wasn't any large boat in the area. He carried a smaller boat with him on the yacht. If he'd carried a, say, sixteen footer with a twenty five or thirty horse kicker and fuel he would arrive at the island somewhere between two and seven thirty tomorrow afternoon, barring trouble. If he'd gone ashore in Sarasota, he'd be here by now. He took his transportation out with him. I figure a kicker no bigger than thirty horse, because weight would be a problem, and those are about the limit a strong person can lift and carry alone.

"A thirty horse, get it in the water and loaded, radio the coast guard with that mayday, fire the boat, and he'd have at least six minutes to get the hell out. Six minutes at around twenty knots. He could've been two or three miles away when the coast guard boat got there. A chopper wouldn't pay attention to some fishing boat a couple miles from a burner.

"The sea's smooth and easy until the tip, then it's been kind of windy, which meant he'd have to slow it to a crawl for the trip down among the islands. It would be much too rough to try to straightline around and across. Considering he'd stop four times for pouring in new fuel and so forth, he'll get here after four. I'd say five thirty to six."

"He might be a hard one to take. After all his perfect planning, he'll be mad as all hell that some stupid cop figured him. Paddy had a bad feeling about this one. So do I."

"He's gonna hole up?"

"I think he'll try something clever or sneaky, myself. We'll have to watch our backsides. He might try to stand us off. I wouldn't put it past him."

They chatted awhile more. Enders was a damned good officer, and was probably a good friend to have. He was like Jim Hill, in that he was the kind you'd like to have along if there was trouble.

The next day was mostly boring. Nick finished the books and walked around a lot. After supper, Enders went back to the spot with him. It was seven ten when they parked.

It was seven fourteen when a light turned on in the house.

Chapter eight

Enders grinned and asked if they should go right on in or wait to see if anyone else showed up. Nick didn't expect anyone else. Enders gave him a walky-talky and suggested he'd go around the back to be ready to tag Posten when he went out that way.

Nick started to move the car, then stopped.

"What?" Enders asked.

"Look at the house." Enders studied it a few minutes, then shrugged.

"No curtains or blinds, so you can see right inside. Lights came on in three rooms at exactly the same time. That might be because there's a master that was turned off, but there's another item here that makes me wonder if maybe this is another clever trick to find if there might be someone watching the place."

"No shadows. No one turned off the lights in one or two of the rooms. There's no one moving in there."

"So *we* wait! It does mean there's a hole in our surveillance, somehow."

"Yeah. He went in to put the timer on the lights sometime in the last hour or so. How long will he wait?"

"Probably all night. He'll go in tomorrow morning, if no one seems interested in those lights. Shall we get a good night's sleep and come back around ten in the morning? He should feel secure enough, by then. I think I'd rather handle it in the light, personally. It's not so easy to move around."

They headed back to Key West.

"Okay. You go around on the beach side. I'll go ring his doorbell. He's never seen me that I know of. He shouldn't suspect anything. I don't think he's particularly dangerous, but he did shoot Downs. I could be wrong. I've spent most of my time on this case being wrong!"

"I brought vests, but he shot Downs in the head, which makes them as much as useless. Be careful. Do *not* take chances."

"You got it! Let's move!"

Enders went around to the beach side, where he began walking toward the house. Nick drove up to park in the oyster shell drive, which would block any car in the garage from getting out and went to ring the doorbell.

Suzanne answered the door, said, "You?!" and tried to slam it. Nick put his foot in the doorsill like the old brush salesman's technique and shoved. She turned and ran for the back. Nick stayed low, and went after her.

This was another thing that didn't make sense! Why didn't he kill her when he killed Downs? What the hell was *she* doing down there?

She went out the back door and into Enders' arms. Nick went through the house, but Posten wasn't there.

"Okay. Where is he?" Enders asked, pushing Suzanne into the big overstuffed chair in the Florida room.

"Who?" she asked, with wide-eyed innocence.

"Downs was shot in the back of the head before the boat was fired. *That* act will get *you* the chair! We *know* you and Downs were on the boat. We can't prove anyone else was, if you clam. Think it over *very* carefully!"

"Yeah!" Enders added. "Meaning if you claim he wasn't there there isn't any jury in the world who would allow you the argument of reasonable doubt."

"But I don't know what the hell you're talking about! Fired what boat?"

"I was right there at the house when you and Downs got aboard your fancy boat and it left the dock. It never came near another dock or shore until the mayday call. We can prove that you and Downs were aboard that vessel. He was shot in the back of the head, so he didn't commit suicide.

"That leaves you – and a murder one charge.

"You went to a great deal of trouble to not be seen as you came here to a house he bought long before the murder of Mathews in your insurance fraud scheme.

"It's interesting, isn't it? You give him to us or you get the chair. I believe it's your move?"

"I had a friend bring me here from Naples! We went to Miami to shop, then she dropped me off on her way to Key West. I don't know what you're talking about!" She sneered. "I wasn't on any boat!"

"What's the friend's name?" Enders asked.

"Norma Gerrard."

"Where's she staying in Key West?" Enders asked.

"How would I know? She said she's meeting someone here and they're going on a cruise."

"What kind of car does she drive?" Nick asked.

"A Taurus. Dark blue."

"What does she look like?" Enders asked.

"About my height. Brownish hair, except she changes it a lot. Maybe a little heavier."

"Two or four door?"

"What?"

"The Taurus. Two or four door?" Enders fired at her.

"I don't remember."

"You went shopping in Miami and drove all this way and you don't even know how many doors the car had?" Enders shot back, quickly. "You put whatever you bought over the seat?"

"We put it in the trunk. It was a two door. I remember now."

"Did you buy much?" Nick asked.

"No. We just shopped. I bought some groceries for here. I got some bread and eggs and that kind of stuff." she replied, gaining confidence.

"When did you arrive?" Nick asked.

"Yesterday afternoon. Four thirty or five."

"She let you out at the street or park in the drive?" Enders asked.

"She came into the damned driveway! I had groceries! I wasn't going to carry all that stuff in from the road!"

"I see," Nick said, silkily. "She drove you here from Miami in her invisible blue Taurus and pulled into the driveway about four thirty or five yesterday afternoon. Now she's going on a cruise with someone you don't know, so we can't ask her to substantiate your alibi.

"You want to try it again? I was watching the place all day yesterday and a bit into the night. No Taurus or anything else pulled into that driveway yesterday – at any time!"

She glared at him. "Kiss my ass!"

"Okay. You are under arrest on the charge of murder in the first degree," Enders said. "You have the right to...."

"I know my rights! Such as the right for you to *not* be here without a warrant!"

Nick grinned and waved a warrant to search the place under her nose. "Oh, we wouldn't be here without that. You'll have to testify against him in court, then we get him and have you as an accessory, anyhow. All you're doing here is giving him a little time. No matter what, we've got you. Protect him, if you think it'll do him any good, but it won't.

"You do understand? I wasn't bluffing about that murder one charge."

"I really don't think I'll want to testify against my *husband* in your court! I already said I know my rights!"

"Poston's not your husband. You never got around to finalizing the annulment proceedings papers from someone named Standing. You can refuse to testify against *him,* if you like.

"Let's get this place thoroughly searched, John. You can cuff her to something solid."

They searched the place carefully, finding a purse with

over fifty thousand dollars in it, but not much else. There was no sign Posten had been there. There were no prints on the timer they found on the breaker box, but he would have wiped it clean. Suzanne seemed to be getting steadily more frightened, but because Nick and Enders kept bringing up that she could get the chair for Downs if Posten wasn't found soon. Nick told Enders it looked like the little lady was finally figuring out that she was set up to be Posten's goat.

They finally sealed the house tight and took Suzanne in for booking. Nick would take her back to Naples, but he wanted to know where Posten was hiding – and where was all that money he'd collected?

"I think we're overlooking something obvious again," Nick said, over his umpteenth cup of coffee. "We have to figure it out! Where is Posten – and where is the money?"

Enders looked puzzled and shrugged Nick started giggling. Enders raised an eyebrow.

"How did they *get* to the island?"

"Oh, hell! On a boat! I had the MP and Coast Guard Patrol looking for them, so didn't watch much, myself. Posten and Suzanne stayed on the boat four days, she goes to the house to decoy us if we're watching for him. He stays on the boat another day or two. It worked."

"We have to find that boat! It was beached somewhere around the island and she walked to the house from it. It wasn't very far. She *did* carry some groceries from it, and she *did....*"

"... stop on an inner island to *buy* those groceries!" Enders finished. "How? They were *all* being watched!"

"Yeah! For a boat with one man in it. I think it'll still be fairly close. We can probably find where it was beached."

They got in the car and headed back to the island. The 16' fiberglass boat was among some mangroves in a little indentation about two hundred yards north of the house. There were fourteen empty six gallon cans, plus the two six gallon tanks the thirty five horse motor used. One of the engine's tanks was down about two and a half gallons.

"They got gas at Cannonball Key," Enders said. "That would make it about right, but where is he?"

"Probably on Cannonball Key. He took the money off and sent her here to find out if we knew about the place. She was to go back after him. We have to go to Cannonball Key."

"We'll take my rig. It's a lot faster and easier by water."

"We'll take this one. He might see it coming and come out to meet us."

"Good show! One of us can stay out of sight until we're there. It's windy enough and there's enough rain that the one piloting would be wearing a slicker and hood."

They worked the boat out of the mangroves and out into the close shallow channel and were quickly moving around the island toward the northwest. It took them nearly three quarters of an hour to reach Cannonball Key, where they docked by the pumps. Enders greeted the dock man and introduced Nick.

"Weeds, this boat stopped here day before yesterday for gas, I think," Enders said.

"I 'member ut."

"There was a man and a woman aboard," Enders went on. "The man took some packages or luggage or something out, and is still on the island?"

"Nup! T'warn't no man. Jist tha woman. Looker. Hooker type, but a looker."

"So! Did the woman take anything out of the boat and leave it anywhere on the island?" Nick asked.

"Yup."

"Do you have any idea where she took it?" Enders asked.

"Post office, I reckon. T'wer all wrapped fer mailin'."

"What kind of package was it?" Nick asked.

"Box. Mebbe a foot by two. Sorta heavyish-like, the way

she uz carryin' ut."

"Brown paper wrap?" Enders asked.

"Huh! Fancy white paper. Slick paper."

"Check this rig, will you?" Enders asked. "I don't know if she oiled it right. Don't want to get stuck out there if she didn't bother with maintenance."

"Yuh-huh. Didn't seem the type to have any sense."

Nick and Enders walked to the end of the dock and over to the little post office in the store. Weeds' wife, Sarah, said she remembered the package, because it seemed odd that some floozie would want to mail anything from the island. She'd mentioned to the postmaster at Key West that there was something awfully fishy about it.

"He'll have the dogs sniff ut," she said. "Prolly a wad 'a drugs'd choke a horse in ut, ya aks me!

"Thut right, Johnny?"

"No," Nick replied. "It'll have something over ten or twelve million dollars in cash in it, I think."

"Saints! Ut right, Johnny?"

"Yep!"

"But where the hell is Posten *now*?!" Nicks spat. "Where was the package to go?"

"On'y over ter Arrerhead Key. Thut's what din make no sense!"

They radioed Key West to be told the package would go out in the following morning's delivery. It was a registered and insured package. A signature would be required.

"How much was it insured for?" Nick asked.

"One thousand. It's not drugs. The dogs don't seem interested. X-ray shows nothing but paper or something."

"Ut's ten million. Cash," Sarah said.

"We..! Are you certain? We can't allow anyone access to a package until signatory has assigned their authorization."

"Who is the addressee?" Enders asked.

"A Mrs. Susan Standing, care of Parker, Arrowhead Key,

fifty one. Let's see. Anyone inside the house may sign for it, but you're on shaky ground, legally, if you open it.

"Can I come ... I guess not. It has to be delivered to the house?" Nick asked.

"That, or to Mrs. Standing, personally, if she has the proper legal identification."

"Thanks," Nick replied. "I'll be at the house to accept it tomorrow, then I'll take it to her and let her open it. She can get one more look at what she killed at least one ... one man for.

"I'll be damned!"

"It'll be out there by nine in the morning," the postmaster said. They said their goodbyes and hung up.

"What was that look for?" Enders asked.

"He was on that boat with her when it left the Naples area, and he was *not* aboard when she got gas at Cannonball Key. What's between here and Naples?"

"I'm unfamiliar with the area, but there's nowhere to stop south of Chokaloskee."

"They did *not* stop there. Posten's feeding the crabs somewhere between here and Naples."

They went back to Arrowhead Key. Nick took his rental to Key West while Enders brought the boat in. They had a good dinner and agreed to meet in the morning at headquarters. When Nick had the package for Suzanne to open.

Nick went to a small bar to listen to a live band and have a beer, then walked back to his motel for the night. He was sure Suzanne would break down and tell them all about it. Tomorrow was going to be a hectic day.

Interesting, but hectic.

"Hi, Suzanne! Have a good night here?" Nick greeted, when she was brought into the room. The sheriff and Enders were there with him.

"Up your stu...!" she began, then stared at the box on the

table.

"Want to take a last look at it?" Enders asked. "It's what you're going to the chair for."

"You can't open it! I know my rights!"

"We can't open it without a court order," Enders said. "We can have one in ten minutes for this one, I flat guarantee you. You can produce Posten for us or you can watch us open the parcel. If there's cash in there, we have a motive that no jury could deny. We won't let you plea bargain if you don't co-operate. It's all over, and you know it!"

She suddenly broke down and started sobbing almost hysterically. Enders raised the eyebrow at Nick. The sheriff started to move to give her a tissue, saw Nick shake his head, and stopped.

"Hot strong coffee anyone?" Nick asked as he unconcernedly poured himself a cup. "Sheriff? John? Suzanne?"

"Black," Enders said.

"Cream and two," the sheriff said.

"Suzanne?" Nick asked.

"You son of a bitch!"

"Coffee?" he asked, unperturbed. "A Mr. Charles LeGrand in New Orleans said you thought more of your acting ability than anyone else did. I tend to agree."

"Black. I guess I always knew it couldn't work."

She ripped the top off the package and slid it across to the sheriff, who opened it. It was packed solidly with hundred dollar bills.

"How much?" Nick asked.

"I don't know. Several million."

Nick sighed deeply. They'd have to count it for the records, but, considering the weight and volume, he could calculate twelve million five to thirteen million.

"So. Where did you leave Posten's body?" Nick asked.

"He's on some little mangrove island where we stopped to spend the night. Just before I started going east, so near the tip. It has a big oyster shell bank. It's about a half mile or so long, I guess. Maybe a hundred feet wide.

"He isn't dead. By the time he gets here from there he'll know better than to come after me. I can finger him for killing Wayne and that bum. He knows I have all that put away."

"You can definitely prove that he killed Wayne Downs and Don Mathews?" Nick asked. "How?"

"I have a tape thing of him telling me and Wayne how we could get millions when he faked the car accident. I think it was mostly Wayne's idea from the first, because Wayne came to New Orleans when I told him there was some guy there who looked just like the picture he had of Lyle." She was talking – and thinking – in a sort of jerky odd-pause fashion. "See, I'd never seen Lyle before, just the picture. Wayne said a little plastic surgery and nobody could tell it wasn't Lyle. I got kind of suspicious when Wayne had Don getting all that work on his teeth and stuff.

"Anyhow, Don got in some trouble and left. I didn't think anything about it, then he ended up dead, and Lyle was bragging about making millions. Wayne talked me into marrying Lyle, who I really did like a lot. He said Lyle always liked real sexy women. I could marry him and get all the money I'd ever be able to spend. He'd still be there for, you know, being my real husband and all.

"It worked out really great! I really did have a whole lot of money to spend, and Lyle is a really good, you know, for the sex thing. When you started poking around I knew you'd find it wasn't Lyle who was dead, you know? I mean, the O. J. trial and all that DNA and that kind of stuff.

"See, I knew Wayne was in the dead thing, so we could get in all kinds of trouble. I wanted to just go away with what we already had ready, but Lyle wouldn't, and Wayne was scared of Lyle by then. When you came and told me you knew Lyle was still alive and we would get caught. Wayne claimed you didn't have anything that would prove anything. All we had to do was sit tight. You thought Lyle ran off to some other country where you couldn't touch him.

"When you came over and said somebody tried to kill him at the place where he was hiding, Wayne said it had hit the fan and we had to get out fast. We took some stuff and got the boat. We could go over to Cancun until the heat died down. I never did figure who tried to kill Lyle!"

"Nobody. He set that up so he could fake his death after killing you and Downs," Nick said.

"Well, we got the boat and started out, and there he was! Already on the boat! I said how we could all stay together now, because he could go to Cancun with us. He told me he had the place down here, which I knew about because some papers came to the house and I knew he was L. L. Small of four thirty two Hutton Place, and I opened it.

"I didn't like the way he was acting, so I turned on my tape recorder, which I always carry in my purse so Wayne can see what I already told the cops so we could keep our story straight.

"Lyle took a gun and shot Wayne in the head! I was never so scared in my life! He looked at me and I said it was a relief to be rid of Wayne because he was nothing but trouble and a wimp.

"See, I knew Lyle wouldn't hurt me if I made him think he was who I really wanted.

"Anyhow, Lyle said we could scuttle the boat and take the outboard down here. He already had gas and food and stuff aboard, because he planned to do it all along, and knew Wayne would try to run in the boat because he planted the idea all along to. He kept telling him it was ready for them to go to Cancun if it got too hot there.

"We started the fire and Lyle said there was a propane tank that was set to blow the boat up and we called the coast guard and said the boat was on fire, then we got out. I got him to stop so we could stretch and use the bathroom and all that twice a day, and we stopped in places like that at night. The last stop was that island. I went to the bathroom and got back on the boat when I said I was going to have sandwiches while we were there and he went to the bathroom.

"I pushed the boat out and had started it up and he came running out, but I was already going and he shot at me, but I stayed real low and just kept going. He had the loran settings all written down and where to turn which direction and all that. I went right to the gas place. I wrapped the money in that box and mailed it to me from there. That's about it."

"Where's the tape?" Enders asked.

"One's in with the money, right there. The other's in my desk drawer back home. I didn't kill anybody! I swear! I didn't even *know* about that until it was too late!"

"If what you say is on those tapes, you saved your life by telling us," Nick said. "I guess we'll have to go after Posten. I wonder if he's still there?"

He was.

"Well, Nick! This is the first one where all your box chart did was confuse the issue!" Marsha said.

They had come from the trial, where Lyle Posten was convicted of murder in the first degree. The jury's unanimous verdict read, "Without recommendation of mercy."

"Well, that was because none of the vast store of information on it had anything to do with the stupid case," Paddy argued. "Nick seems always to end up with the cases that don't make any sense. We're pretty much used to it now.

"The women have Frog and Dolly's wedding all planned and ready to go. I'll never understand why they refuse to allow Frog any say in it! It *is* his wedding!"

"Pancho said it best," Jim answered. "So long as the bridegroom is presentable, he's merely one of the details.

"Lonnie's brat's due any day now."

"It was due two days ago!" Marsha shot back. "She just *can't* get her schedule straight!

"What'll happen to that silly whorish woman, now? She was an accessory, no matter how you slice it."

"What would you say her IQ is?" Paddy asked.

"Maybe the same as her age," Marsha replied. "I'd say twenty seven or eight. No more!"

"She was just a stupid bimbo they used," Jim said.

"No. She was in on a lot of the fraud," Nick replied. "The charity scams, not the insurance stuff. Until later.

"She'll get some probation as part of the plea deal for her testimony and those tapes."

"What else does she get out of it? Those stupid crooked advertising companies?" Marsha asked.

"No," Paddy replied. "Posten had bankrupted all of them when he grabbed the money. They're history. She's got a job offer in New Orleans. A talent agency wants her on an exclusive.

"You told her not to take it, Nick?"

"She had me read the offer. It would make her story their exclusive property. She'll probably write a book and collect a million or two and live happily ever after."

"Yeah! Until some other smart con man ropes her into another stupid get rich quick and crooked scheme!" Marsha snapped.

"Nope! No such deals! I told her to make LeGrand her exclusive agent. She doesn't do a single thing without his consent."

"Why?" Marsha asked.

"Because he works weekends and nights to get jobs for people with little or no talent. He gets jobs for talented people like Mathews, who are as hopeless. He gives them some hope that they can make something of themselves. He's honest. The percentage from her book will give him a little something for his years of trying.

"Face it! The lowest dregs of modern society write books and make umpty millions. Nobody profits but *them*! It's the American way! Crime pays! Big! Write a book!

"It's gonna happen, anyhow. Why not let some poor schnook who's trying to help somebody else get a percent of the rake-off?"

"Ah-ha!" Paddy cried. "Those insurance companies want to give you a lot of money for what you saved them! You don't fool me with all this altruistic sludge! You can't take it, you know."

"No, but Cole can! They've set up a college fund for him, held strictly in trust that I can't touch, even if I would."

"How much is in it?" Marsha asked.

"Eighty six thousand," Nick answered.

"Oh, wow! By the time Cole gets to college, which is about fifteen years down the line, that won't buy his first semester books!" Jim said.

"It might buy his books," Nick shot back. "I've been putting enough for his tuition away from my bloated salary and all those bribes!"

"Bribes? How does a homicide cop get to collect bribes – and how did I miss that?" Marsha asked. "What's this crap about a bloated salary? The only thing that's bloated around here is your stupid ego!"

"*My* ego? Oh, really, Specialist Blevins? You never did tell us a specialist *what*!"

This would probably deteriorate into quite a raucous joke and insult session.

It did.

C. D. Moulton's works are available on most major outlets as printed or e-books. CD writes the CD Grimes, PI, mysteries, the Det. Lt. Nick Storie mysteries, the Clint Faraday mysteries, the Flight of the Maita science fiction series, books on orchid culture and many others of many types. Mystery, adventure, intrigue, science fiction, humor, fantasy, paranormal, mild erotica, and factual.